SOUTHPAW

FRANK KING

LYNX BOOKS

New York

Special thanks to Susan Anne Protter, Judith Stern,
Ragnhild Hayen, and David M. Harris

SOUTHPAW

ISBN: 1-55802-000-4

First Printing/July 1988

This book is published by Lynx Books, a division of Lynx Communications, Inc., 41 Madison Avenue, New York, New York, 10010.
The name "Lynx" together with the logotype consisting of a stylized
head of a lynx is a trademark of Lynx Communications, Inc.

Printed in the United States of America

0 9 8 7 6 5 4 3 2 1

Cover painting by Michael Kanarek
Edited by Gwendolyn Smith

When I have inspired universal horror and disgust, I shall have conquered solitude.

—CHARLES BAUDELAIRE

I don't care what color that sonofabitch is. He blocked the bag.

—ENOS SLAUGHTER, ST. LOUIS CARDINALS, RESPONDING TO CHARGES OF RACISM AFTER HE BLOODILY SPIKED JACKIE ROBINSON IN 1949

SOUTHPAW

1

JUST north of the California-Oregon border and just east of the Coast Range lies the city of Oaktown. Settled originally in 1823, it has seen miners, loggers, ranchers, millers, and manufacturers rise and fall as economic masters. But by the mid-1980's the city had settled into a viable but precarious economic balance of aerospace plants, two well-attended junior colleges, and the West Coast headquarters of the world's fourth-largest direct-mail marketing company.

It is a city whose history is always being ploughed under because of economic fluctuations—railroads vanished, roads appeared, factories collapsed, buildings burned.

Even the city's many ethnic groups—Italians, Czechs, Finns, etc.—seem to vanish in marriage or exile.

Oaktown has sent many young men to many wars and many more of its young men and women to Eugene and San Francisco and Los

Angeles to pursue careers and mates and "experience". It is not a famous city, although it has produced a famous hybrid rose named after it . . . a very effective low-level, carrier-based bomber . . . some con men and murderers . . . a few Broadway actresses.

Oaktown is hard to categorize, hard to forget, hard to get through on any late afternoon if you are driving.

But there is one fact, one thing, one tradition that has given this struggling, changing city of some 395,000 souls an anchor that never shifted, a fulcrum on which to vent their woes and their joys—the Oaktown Wolves, their baseball team.

For more than forty years the Oaktown Wolves have represented the city in the august Pacific Coast League; the league that was the jewel of the minor leagues; the league that produced Joe DiMaggio and Kiner and hundreds of other great ballplayers; the league that was, in its heyday, very close to major-league caliber.

In the 1950's, the PCL had fought tooth and nail to prevent the move of the Dodgers and the Giants to the West Coast. They lost that battle and many of their California franchises. But the PCL survived and, after a few lean decades, was now thriving again in cities like Phoenix, Las Vegas, Portland, Vancouver, Tucson, Calgary, and others.

It didn't matter that Oaktown was the smallest city in the PCL, was not affiliated with any major-league team, paid the lowest salaries, and traditionally had the sorriest collection of has-beens and youngsters—the Wolves were always in the hunt one way or the other. They fought and scrapped and hit and ran and played their own brand of baseball.

The team—the Wolves—was the creation of one man, Walter Bunsen, who had parlayed two dirt-moving machines into a multimillion-dollar contracting firm.

Bunsen was an autocrat and a miser, and he ran the team that way; firing three or four managers a season, demanding that he have complete control over strategy and pitching rotation, doing everything and listening to no one.

He died in the fall of 1963. All his life, residents of Oaktown had either hated him or held him in contempt—but when he died he was a universal hero.

How did this remarkable transformation take place? Two months before Walter Bunsen died, the Oaktown Wolves had done the impossible— they had won the championship of the Pacific Coast League—the first and last time that ever happened.

And they won it after being in last place at the season's halfway mark; then making the most miraculous comeback in league history and winning 71 percent of their remaining games.

That year, 1963, became the city of Oaktown's most precious memory. It was an event unlike any other in the city's history. And people said that Walter Bunsen died at exactly the right time; with the PCL championship in his back pocket.

People in Oaktown remember what they were

doing in 1963; they remember where they were
sitting, who they were with—when the last out
of the last inning made the Oaktown Wolves the
champions of the Pacific Coast League.

The 1988 season was almost upon Oaktown
now. And this team was being evaluated against
the 1963 team, as was the custom.

The papers were filled with prognostications.
Bewildered young infielders, playing for Oaktown for the first season, were constantly being
pulled into radio stations for interviews. The city,
as they say, was on its toes.

2

FOUR blocks from Bunsen Stadium on Oak-town's Southwest Side, once a grimy industrial area but now leveled into a series of parks, was the bar called Victor's.

At two o'clock in the afternoon, two weeks before the opening game of the season, Dominic Lombardi sat in a far booth, alone, sipping Budweiser from a bottle.

He was past seventy but still as wiry as he was during his playing days with the San Francisco Seals as a teammate of the great Joe DiMaggio. Dominic had made it into the majors for only a week or so, long enough, as he tells it, to have a cup of coffee with the Boston Red Sox.

It was Dominic who had managed the Wolves to their 1963 championship. He no longer coached or managed, but he was still employed by the Wolves' organization.

He was simply "the Coach" to everyone in Oaktown; the man who best personified the spirit of the franchise. He traveled with the team, sat in the owner's box during games, helped plan trades and signings and schedules. He was now a revered jack-of-all-trades.

Dominic still wore one of those old-fashioned, Roger Maris brush haircuts—only there was little black among the gray bristles.

Arthritis had twisted one part of his back and one arm. His fingers had been broken and reset many times—the mark of an old catcher—and his face had seen too much sun—leathery crevices seemed to crisscross in a random pattern.

Dominic stared at the clock. Bunny was already thirty minutes late. In that manner, he realized, Cynthia "Bunny" Bunsen was just like her father. That bastard was always late; he would always make you wait. But that was where the similarity ended.

In fact, Dominic realized, in the five or six years that Bunny had run the team as well as owned it, she had done a damn good job. Sure, sometimes she interfered, and sometimes she was difficult, and there were all those rumors of her having affairs with ballplayers—but on the whole, she knew what she was doing. She studied the game, and she loved it.

Sometimes he was absolutely amazed that she was only twenty-six years old. And anyway, anything was better than the long series of interim general managers the Wolves had experienced between the death of Walter Bunsen and his daughter's finally growing up and coming home

to stay after doing God knows what in God
knows where.

Dominic finished the bottle and grinned. He
remembered clearly Bunny as a newborn baby—
well, about three months old—screaming her
lungs out in an improvised cradle in the cham-
pagne-soaked clubhouse after they had copped in
1963.

It had all come together for Walter Bunsen that
year—a new child and a championship. And then
it had fallen apart as quickly as it came—his
death and, a year later, his wife's death.

The bartender brought him another beer without either of them saying a word. He took a swig,
leaned back, and pressed his shoulders against the
booth to ease the arthritic throbbing.

He heard Bunny before he saw her. She was
arguing with the current Wolves' manager, Roger
Randle. They were both so immersed in their
own points of view that they seemed to have forgotten where Dominic always sat. Finally, they
slid into the booth across from him.

"Ask the Coach. He'll agree with me," Bunny
said while she raised a hand to the bartender,
who hustled over with two more beers, some
glasses, and a couple of bowls of potato chips.

Dominic knew what he was going to be asked.
Bunny wanted Roger to use Turo at third base
for the opener; and Roger wanted Doherty. It
was rare for Bunny to actually butt in like this.
In fact, maybe she was just kidding. She knew
that he, Dominic, wasn't going to cross Roger.
She knew he would agree with Roger's choice.

Roger was the manager, and he was a good baseball man. After all, he had been Dominic's third
baseman on that 1963 championship team—and
he would have made it to the majors, to the Bal-
timore Orioles, if there hadn't been a gentleman
named Brooks Robinson anchored there.

"Well, Coach," said Roger, smiling broadly,
"Turo or Doherty?"

Dominic smiled back at the short, powerfully
built man, now almost bald except for a frizzled
red top.

Then he grinned at Bunny, who was waiting
for his answer while digging through the potato
chips, searching for a perfectly shaped one.

She was wearing a very expensive black suit,
fancy shoes, and carrying a beautiful purse. Her
golden hair was long and hung loose.

Money, looks, and power, Dominic thought,
she has it all. And it was here in Victor's that she
exercised her talents when she wanted to, because, although there was, beneath Bunsen Stadium, a whole suite of offices whose door read
Executive Offices, Oaktown Wolves Baseball
Team—no one ever discussed anything there.

The team was run from Victor's. Dominic liked
that—he always had; there was no more hal-
lowed baseball tradition in the majors or the mi-
nors than running a team from a saloon.

"Well," said Dominic, taking a large and theatrical swallow, "Turo is a crowd-pleaser. He can
hit the ball. But he can't hit righties at all, and
he can't field bunts unless someone rolls him one
down the line."

Bunny waved her hand at him despairingly, signaling that she was dropping the entire argument.

"You're coming to the tryouts, aren't you? They're at five."

At first Dominic couldn't recall what tryouts Bunny was talking about. Then he remembered: Bunny had decided to hire an animal mascot to work home games—like the San Diego Chicken or the Philly Phanatic. It was a good marketing idea, particularly as a way to get small kids into the stadium.

Dominic grimaced and stared at Roger, who shrugged his shoulders as if to say that he could no longer fight progress.

First there had been new uniforms, Dominic thought, and then ball girls, and now a mascot.

"Why do you need me there?" he asked.

"Because you're one of the judges."

"You're kidding," Dominic said, astonished.

"Would I kid the Coach?" she retorted and then excused herself and headed for the ladies' room.

"It'll go quick," Roger promised him, adding, "After all, how many frustrated San Diego Chickens can there be in Oaktown?"

Roger opened a small pack of cheap cigars—panatelas—and handed one to Dominic. The two men took their time peeling the cellophane off and then lighting up.

"How's Woodson coming?" Dominic asked when he had finally lit the cigar.

"The kid'll win fifteen," Roger said.

"If he wins fifteen, we can win it all," Dominic said.

Roger laughed very hard, and then looked up with skeptical eyes at his former manager.

"Like sixty-three?" he asked.

"Screw sixty-three," Dominic retorted.

"The trouble with Woodson is that he can't get off the mound to cover the bases. It takes him about thirty seconds just to unravel. He's like a pretzel. Any ball hit toward first base that Loors can't handle all by himself means a hit with Woodson on the mound."

Dominic nodded in agreement. All the practice drills in the world couldn't teach a kid how to do that. It's an instinct.

Roger leaned over and carefully deposited his ash in the receptacle which carried the logo of the Oaktown Wolves on its side.

An ear-shattering scream suddenly exploded in the bar.

Everyone sat up. No one moved.

The scream came again; this time longer in duration and deeper in intensity.

"My God, it's Bunny," Roger yelled.

He sprinted toward the back where the bathrooms were. Dominic followed, carrying an empty beer bottle, grasping it tightly by the neck.

They barged through the wooden door of the ladies' room, splintering some wood.

Bunny was backed up against the wall, her face pallid with fear.

A hunched-over, disheveled man hovered near her, half leaning against the wall.

Roger punched the man on the side of the face, spinning him around. The sound of knuckle on bone was like a gunshot.

Then Roger smashed him on the back of the neck and the man fell forward, landing on Dominic.

Roger came at him again.

"Wait," Dominic yelled, "it's Jackie Cannon."

Roger stopped, breathing heavily, his eyes wild. Then he turned back to Bunny.

"I'm okay, I'm okay," she said. "I just turned around and there he was, suddenly. He put his hand on my face and I started to scream. Oh God, I was scared."

Dominic said: "He's drunk, Roger. He's drunk as a lord, and he probably thought this was the men's room."

Dominic pulled the man out of the bathroom and into the hallway, then out onto the street by a side door. The man's face was a mass of blood.

Then Dominic propped him up against the wall and held him there.

Roger came out a few moments later, blowing on his fists to ease the pain.

"She's okay," he said. "She thought he was a rapist."

He stared at the bleeding drunk and then added: "I never would have recognized him in a million years, and I played with him."

Dominic loosened his grip on Jackie Cannon's arm. He had heard that the onetime all-star, the driving force behind the 1963 Wolves championship, had come upon hard times; that he was in and out of the joint; that he was broke; that he had gone to Canada.

He had heard all kinds of stories about Jackie Cannon, but what he saw was horrible—a prematurely aged, sloppy, filthy derelict.

"What do we do?" Roger asked.

"Leave him be," Dominic said.

They both reached into their pockets, extracted their loose singles, and shoved them into Cannon's side pocket. He stared dumbly at them and slid to the ground.

3

THE whole city had been invited, free of cost, to attend the mascot tryouts—but only about five hundred came. They were scattered throughout the seats behind home plate and fanned out on the first- and third-base sides of the diamond. Many of those attending were obviously family and friends of the contestants.

The judges' table was set right on the field in front of the dugout. There were nine judges in all: Bunny, Dominic, Roger, the chairman of the drama department at one of the junior colleges, and five city politicians—including the mayor, a municipal judge, and the fire commissioner.

Contestants changed into their outfits in the clubhouse, like ballplayers, then came out of the dugout and climbed on top of it to perform so that they could be seen very clearly by everyone in the stadium, no matter where they were.

It was beginning to get dark, and the lights were turned on. A slight, chilled drizzle began to fall.

Each contestant was required to perform a five-minute routine. The first one was a duck; then there was a goose, a fox, a wolf, a bat, a hawk, and a few that were totally unrecognizable.

It was like a very pleasant lunatic asylum had been emptied, and the inmates were appearing one by one dressed in their best fantasy garb. A fox pulled out a live chicken and started to tango with it. A bat bared his ferocious teeth, perked up his ears, and flew off the top of the dugout, only to crash-land unceremoniously two seconds later. A few acts even spilled over onto the field, like the duck who dove into home plate thinking it was a pond!

Some were funny, some stupid, some exotic. But what they all were about, ultimately, was enthusiasm—for a team and a city. The people in the stands knew that and applauded them.

At the long table, the judges took notes on yellow legal pads.

"How many are there going to be?" Dominic whispered to Roger.

"I don't know. Maybe thousands," Roger answered. The younger man listened to the older man groan. Then he saw Bunny conferring with another judge—both of them appearing to treat the nonsense with great seriousness. Bunny had obviously shaken off that ugly incident. She was back in control.

Roger moved closer to Dominic and said, "I can't get over what he looked like."

"Who?"

"Jackie Cannon."

"Indians can't drink. It does something to them. It kills them early."

"Jackie Cannon? Indian?"

"Half Indian. His mother, from Vancouver Island, I think, or one of those islands off the coast. Hell, you played with him. Didn't you know?"

"I wasn't friendly with him. In fact, I thought he was a creep."

"Might have been, but he sure could play."

They returned to their judging, watching the next potential mascot cavort in a bizarre uniform on top of the dugout.

Inside the clubhouse, Julie Novick was waiting for her turn.

On the bench in front of her were laid out three uniforms for her routine. There was the "happy wolf" uniform with a big goofy gap-toothed face. There was the "bad wolf" uniform with a ferocious scowl. And there was the "confused wolf" uniform with a blank, almost lunatic expression that elicited both laughter and affection.

She didn't know which one she would choose for her performance. She had worked very hard on all three costumes, and she knew a good routine for each of them by heart.

If she could do all three, she would win. But there was only one San Diego Chicken, and if she won, there would be only one Oaktown Wolf.

She chose the confused wolf and started putting the suit on.

As the other contestants around her dressed and went out to audition, Julie felt her confidence return. She had spent a lot of time on this; it wasn't a joke or a game or a challenge.

She was doing it for the money.

They would pay the mascot they chose $100 for every home game, and while the San Diego Chicken was getting about $150,000 a year, $100 for a few hours' work was a gold mine for Julie Novick.

She already held two jobs—one after school and the other on weekends. Her mother needed the money also; so did her brothers and sisters.

Even crazy Matt, who was two years older than she and had just come home from jail—even he needed money; and she would give him some if she got the mascot job even though she was deathly afraid of him.

Ever since the father was killed in a trucking accident, the Novick family had been having trouble making ends meet—paying rent, buying food, meeting the payments for the medical insurance, everything.

Julie slid the wolf's head over her own, fastening it carefully to the rest of the suit. Her fingers were beginning to tremble. She was getting nervous. There was a lot at stake.

Fifteen minutes later the audience and the judges were howling with laughter as they watched a very confused wolf standing upright on top of the dugout trying to understand what a baseball glove was.

The wolf, with one ear twirling around and the other hanging down, had bent over and picked up a fielder's mitt, turned it over and over, and then, perplexed, finally shoved it between his ferocious teeth only to spit it out, even more perplexed. Then the confused wolf turned toward the judges' table to stare at those who were staring at him.

There was something about the costume that made the wolf appear lovable, ferocious, and pathetic all at the same time.

The claws and teeth glittered with threat (a friendly junk dealer had cut them from scrap metal and Julie had burnished them), but the continuously changing face of the wolf seemed to perpetually blunt the threat. It was a wolf to be loved.

Julie exited to prolonged applause. Eleven more contestants came out after she did, and then the judges gathered and compared notes. They wrote down their first and second choices on the yellow pads, then the sheets were ripped off the pads and collected.

The audience in the stands buzzed with anticipation; each claque was calling out the name of its favorite.

In the last row behind home plate, far out on the right-field side, Jackie Cannon huddled—a bottle of cheap red table wine in a paper bag next to him.

He stared down the lines; this was not the stadium he had played in so many years ago. Nothing in the stadium was familiar.

Jackie Cannon did not understand what was happening on the field. It looked like a circus—people in strange costumes were jumping from the dugout to the field, back and forth.

He saw the table with the judges, but he couldn't make out their faces. His own face was still bloodied from the bar. He didn't remember much of what happened. It all seemed strange now, although he knew he had been there for a purpose. He did remember seeing Roger and Dominic. Why had they turned against him? Why had she screamed in the bathroom?

Suddenly there was a roar from the crowd. Jackie saw someone pop out of the dugout. He took a long pull of the red wine. He started applauding too. Then his eyes focused. It wasn't a person. It was an animal. It was a wolf.

The stadium loudspeaker suddenly went on. A voice boomed out.

"Ladies and gentlemen. We are pleased to announce, by unanimous vote of the judges, a new mascot for the Oaktown Wolves—Julie Novick!"

Standing in front of the judges' table, holding the wolf's head in one hand, Julie acknowledged the cheers.

Jackie Cannon started to tremble, turning his face away, digging desperately in his shredded pockets. He pulled out a strange object—three shells strung together on a string.

Grasping one part of the string with all his fingers, he shook the object and the shells came together in a rattle . . . a dull, clicking rattle. No one in the stadium heard it or saw it.

4

"WELL, Coach, here we go again," Bunny said.

Dominic picked up the small orange-juice glass and saluted the toast. They were seated in the poshest restaurant in Oaktown, The Grill at the Hotel Croyden.

It had become a tradition for Bunny and Dominic to have breakfast there on the morning of opening day. And at seven-thirty that evening the Oaktown Wolves would open the season against Portland in Bunsen Stadium.

At eight-thirty in the morning the restaurant was filled with people. Dominic loved a good breakfast—particularly the buckwheat pancakes topped with one egg over that The Grill was famous for. He loved the way they served the syrup: in elaborate silver mugs with a spout shaped like a dolphin. It was hokey, but he liked it.

"You know, Coach, it's funny, but every time I start a new season I feel that I really knew my

father, that I somehow talked to him, that I grew
up with him. Do you know what I mean?"

"Your father and you would have got along
just fine," Dominic lied.

In fact, he knew that Bunny was far too independent to take the kind of shit that her father
was always handing out.

He remembered how he had learned to survive
while managing for Walter Bunsen. He didn't say
a word in response to anything Walter Bunsen
said to him. Walter cursed him . . . Walter
screamed at him . . . Walter insulted him . . .
Walter begged him . . . Dominic just refused to
rise to the bait. And finally, finally, Walter Bunsen began to treat him like a human being. And
then he died. Dominic laughed grimly at the
memory of their confrontations.

"What are you laughing at?" Bunny asked,
suddenly insulted, thinking Dominic was laughing at her.

"The pancakes," Dominic answered quickly,
pointing to his bulging stomach. "I don't need
pancakes."

She leaned across the table and patted his
hand; a beautiful young woman playing with an
old man. "Eat, Coach, it's going to be a long
day."

And surely it would be a long day. For when
they left the breakfast table Bunny and Dominic
would have to begin the long chain of opening-
day ceremonies—from the obligatory stop at the
mayor's office to the local public high school and
then to a few luncheons and the grand parade.

Dominic loathed opening day. He never understood how it had become like a college football homecoming day with banners and bands. That was not what baseball was about.

But he always went because Bunny demanded it; no, she didn't really demand it, she expected it and he couldn't say no.

"You would think they would know how to buy grapefruit here," Bunny said petulantly as she dug into the half grapefruit in front of her, grimacing at the sourness of it.

Dominic grinned. What made Bunny so charming was her mask as a child-woman; one moment she would act like a six-year-old girl and the next moment she would act like the chief operating officer of a corporation.

She was disarming, always at least two steps ahead of you.

Sometimes he felt uneasy about the relationship that had developed between them. He was her surrogate father in one sense. He was also her romantic model of what an old ballplayer should be.

Deep inside he knew he was neither. But she was the closest thing he had to family, and she and she alone was his meal ticket. He never had made any money at all and he could never save a dime.

He couldn't do anything but play baseball when he was young, manage a baseball team when he was middle-aged, and, now that he was old, the only thing he could do was latch on to someone like Bunny, who respected and loved what he had been.

She finally pushed the grapefruit away.

"Remember that night in the bar when I started to scream?" she asked. Dominic nodded.

"God, did I act the little fool! Screaming rape when it was only a drunk who couldn't read which room was for which gender."

She laughed and added: "Maybe I need a vacation."

And then she asked: "Who was that drunk, anyway?"

"Just a drunk," Dominic lied. He didn't think he should go into the sad life of Jackie Cannon. And besides, he didn't really know what had happened in the bar except for the ending.

"You know, Coach," Bunny said, changing the topic, and with excitement rising in her voice. "Whenever we start the season, that very day, opening day, I always get a kind of chill at the base of my spine—a feeling that *this* year, not next year, is going to be 1963 again; that it's all going to come together; that we're going to blow the league away."

Her sudden, almost explosive enthusiasm made her uncomfortable, embarrassed. She reached into the pocket of her coat, which was draped over the chair, for a cigarette. It was an old habit—she had stopped smoking three years ago. Her fingers found something in the pocket. She winced. It was that stupid cheap necklace she had found there a few days ago. She didn't know where it had come from. It wasn't the type of jewelry she would buy for herself. She made a mental note to throw it away as soon as possible.

Dominic popped the last piece of pancake into his mouth, chewed it, drank some water, sipped some coffee, and then said: "You never know, you never know."

He sat back. It was the smell of opening day he had always loved, from the day he started playing to the day he packed it in—the smell of new game uniforms being broken out for the first time . . . the smell of the freshly painted dugout steps. The memories began to flood his mind.

Five miles south of the Hotel Croyden, in the Novick family's small, almost squalid wooden house, Julie Novick had begun to lay out her equipment for her debut as the Oaktown Wolf, the new mascot of the team. Even though the opening-day ceremonies were many hours away, she wanted to be ready, absolutely ready.

The costumes, all three of them, had been packed in boxes in the closet, awaiting the big day.

Then her mother called her down for breakfast. She went, reluctantly, and had just bread and butter and jam and a cup of tea.

Matt was there, leering at her, making fun of her. Her mother told Matt to shut up, and he did.

Julie wished he would move out like he was always threatening to do. Everybody said that Matt had been in jail because he had sexually molested a young girl, but Julie never knew the complete story because her mother would not speak of it.

When she was finished she ran back upstairs to finish unpacking the costumes.

To her horror, she realized that one of the costumes had vanished: bad wolf had vanished.

It was the confused wolf costume that had won her the job, but she wanted the other ones for backup, just in case something happened or the thing wasn't going over; if she laid a very large egg, she could always switch to one of the other costumes.

This was a job she could not afford to screw up—the money and the opportunities were too good.

Frenzied, she emptied the closet completely, then the hall closet, then searched under the beds.

She screamed downstairs to her mother, who came up and helped her look. The costume was gone.

"Maybe you left it at the stadium during one of your practice sessions," her mother suggested.

Julie shook her head. She hadn't left it there. She knew she had brought them all home.

"Put up a note on the bulletin board there, in the office at the stadium," her mother suggested.

Julie sat down on the bed, suddenly exhausted and weepy. She stared out the window. It was a bright sunny morning. The drizzle had burned away, though it probably would be back.

"Matt took it," she said slowly, not looking at her mother.

"You don't know that, Julie. That's crazy. Why would Matt take one of your costumes?"

"Because he's crazy and he hates me and he's jealous of me."

Her mother didn't answer.

"Oh God, Mom, I wish he had never come home."

Her mother sat down on the bed beside Julie and put her arm around her.

"Please don't say that, Julie. He's your brother. He loves you. He loves all of us. We'll find the costume. It's not the one you need for tonight. Everything will be okay, Julie. Believe me."

A mile west of the Novick house, nestled in the dip between two wooded hills, was Revell Street, and at the foot of Revell Street was the large brick house of one of the city's most successful surgeons: Harry Draught.

At noon on that day, he drove his daughter, Alice Draught, to Bunsen Stadium.

Alice was seventeen years old, but she had tried out for one of the ball girl jobs and won it even though it was usual for the ball girls to be sixteen years old, or younger.

There were only two ball girls for each game; one stationed just past third base on the left-field line, close to the stands, and the other stationed just past first base, on the right-field line.

They wore full uniforms and were armed with particularly large gloves. Their job was simply to either catch or run down foul balls, collect the balls, and get them back to the dugout.

Dr. Draught stayed with his daughter as she and the other girl received their instructions from the team's equipment manager, Moe Dallek.

Moe reminded the girls that baseballs are expensive and they shouldn't throw the balls into the stands no matter how the fans begged for them. He told them they weren't getting paid to make great stops of hard line drives so they should be very careful out there.

Then he went briefly into the gymnastic element. A tradition had developed that the ball girls for the Oaktown Wolves were gymnasts as well, and after certain ball retrievals the girls would do cartwheels and other stunts, much to the roaring approval of the fans.

Alice Draught was an excellent gymnast. Very small, very light, very wiry, her blond ponytail secured with thick rubber bands, she was determined to really give them a show out there.

Maybe it was the glint in her eye that made Moe waggle one finger at her, after winking at her father, and say: "One catch, one cartwheel, okay?"

The two girls giggled and their fathers took them away. They would bring the girls back to the ballpark at seven P.M., a half hour before game time.

"Get dressed at home," was Moe's parting advice.

At two in the afternoon the main event of the opening-day ceremonies began: the parade from Bunsen Stadium to City Hall.

The order of march was always the same. In

front were the two police officers on horseback—
which constituted one half of the city's entire
mounted troop.

Then the city's largest fire engine with the fire
department mascot, a beautiful and much loved
Dalmation named Sarge.

After that came the first line, including Bunny
Bunsen, Dominic, any priests and ministers who
could be rounded up, a few city officials, and
once in a while a representative from the state
government.

Then came the floats and the public and parochial high schools' marching bands; and after
them came the ballplayers, riding in convertibles
along with the manager, Roger Randle, the
trainer, the groundskeepers, and everyone even
remotely connected to the team.

This year's parade was exactly the same as all
the others except at the head of the parade, this
year, for the first time, there was a single marching drummer who preceded the prancing police
horses.

The streets along the line of march were filled
with people applauding and shouting encouragement. The sun kept appearing and disappearing
and each new reappearance brought renewed
cheers from the crowd.

Dominic walked wearily beside Bunny, watching the building line so he would know after each
block just how much longer the bloody thing
would last.

When the parade reached the foot of Memorial
Drive and had to make a sharp ninety-degree

turn onto Oregon Avenue—which was the last leg of the trip—everyone had to slow down . . . to almost march in place.

Suddenly, just as Dominic and Bunny were making that turn, they heard one of the police horses emit a bloodcurdling whinny that seemed to come from the center of its body—it was a whinny and a scream and a groan and a plea all wrapped in one. The sound mesmerized the entire parade. Bunny grew pale and grabbed Dominic's arm. She had never heard a sound so horrible in her life.

From where they stood they could see what was happening. The fire department mascot, Sarge the Dalmation, had clamped his teeth viciously onto the horse's flank.

Great spurts of blood were coming from the wound, as if some internal demon were pumping it.

The horse was rearing; the police officer had already been thrown to the ground and was lying there—dazed.

The dog held on, a strange, almost gurgling sound coming from his throat.

The other police officer dismounted and pulled his weapon out of the dress holster. Holding it with two hands, he tried to take aim at the crazed dog who was being whipped back and forth by the crazed horse, but nonetheless managed to hold on.

And then, suddenly, the dog let go.

He stood in the center of the street, legs trembling, jaws flecked with blood, panting heavily.

The dog stared at the police officer, who now came closer.

The dog's entire body began to shake. He lifted up his muzzle once and tried to howl—but it was aborted by the tremors which now seemed to roll through his body in waves.

The dog fell . . . stiffened . . . relaxed . . . and then stiffened and relaxed again.

Then he died right there—suddenly, on the street, next to the wounded horse who remained absolutely still.

Those in the parade and those lined up to watch the parade viewed the strange interlude in silence, as if it were a play performed in their behalf. When it was over, when the dog died, one could feel an enormous discomfort moving from person to person. It was as if the play had been a macabre warning. But to whom? About what?

The incident held up the parade, but it didn't stop it. As they finally got moving again, Bunny whispered to Dominic: "It's a good thing we don't believe in omens, isn't it, Coach?"

Dominic didn't know whether she was being serious or sarcastic, so he just let it pass and marched on.

5

DOMINIC laughed out loud in spite of himself.

Bunny, seated next to him behind the dugout, applauded wildly.

The entire packed stadium reverberated with laughter and applause.

The new mascot, Wolfie, had made its mark a few minutes before game time. Just as Woodson was about to finish his warm-up pitches in the bullpen, the large confused wolf, who was carrying a bucket of water, had ambled out to the Oaktown pitcher.

Julie had practiced this act, and she got it perfectly. Holding up one paw as a signal to the pitcher to stop, she took the ball from his hand, immersed it in the water, and handed it back to him.

This was a real spitball, the mascot seemed to be saying, and you might as well do it right.

The woeful wolf then trundled back across the field to the cheers of the assembled.

The remaining water in the bucket was flung near the first-base umpire, who engaged in a mock battle with the wolf, and the crowd loved that even more. Finally, the wolf lay down on first base and dozed.

The marching band, which had stood quietly during the mascot's routine, began its final circumnavigation of the field, playing a rousing march. Finally, it formed a large "O" for Oaktown in the center of the field. The noise in the stadium grew deafening. Banners were waved. The "Let's Go, Wolves" chant started. Everyone was on their feet ringing in the new season.

Then the game started. Roger started Turo at third, Sisco at short, Battaglia at second, Loors on first, Dwyer in left, Ardmore in center, Secouria in right, and Timken behind the plate.

It was a strong right-handed batting lineup against the Portland left-hander.

Woodson, the Wolves' pitcher, was superb for the first three innings.

And Bunny kept up a running commentary directed at Dominic as if to show him how much she had learned over the years. Dominic was impressed. She had the baseball language down pat. She told him how unique Woodson was; a big strong kid who throws junk. She said Woodson had three pitches—a slow curve, a slower curve, and no curve at all.

Everything she said was right on the mark, and Dominic kept nodding his head in amused agreement, although he had to keep the amusement

masked or she would call him a patronizing old
bastard and resent him.

Woodson, however, got a bit wild in the
fourth, walking two. One went to third on a
passed ball and came home on a sacrifice fly.

Oaktown tied the score at 1-1 in the bottom
of the fifth with a solo home run by Loors—a
towering big-league shot. The place went crazy.

Oaktown wrapped it up in the sixth inning
with a five-run outburst, including back-to-back
doubles.

Roger took out Woodson to a standing ovation
and put in Hendrix to mop up. Hendrix had been
released outright by the Milwaukee Brewers two
years ago after his knee went—but now was
working himself back. When in shape, he had a
wicked slider and pinpoint control.

Now that the game was on ice, or seemed to
be, Dominic hoped Bunny would calm down.
But she kept up the chatter; she kept saying how
wonderful it was, and Dominic could understand
her enthusiasm even though it was only the first
game of the season.

After all, the stands were full and the fans were
cheering every pitch. The mascot idea had
worked out well—the wolf wasn't the San Diego
Chicken but it was very funny. The ball girls
drew "oohs" and "aahs" with their cartwheels after they clumsily trapped the foul balls in their
overstuffed gloves. The fans kept breaking into
chants and songs and waves. And the Wolves
were ahead by five runs.

As the game wore on Julie Novick performed

less and less. That was part of her game plan.
She had studied the San Diego Chicken, and he
also diminished his exposure in the late innings
to avoid overkill. She waited and watched,
crouched by the side of the dugout. Inside the
wolf suit she was sweating profusely. She was
growing tired and her legs ached. Once or twice
during the game she had spotted Bunny Bunsen
in the stands, the golden girl, and she had felt
jealousy and anger at the woman's wealth and
power and sophistication. Julie realized that it
was Bunny's decision to hire a mascot that had
enabled her to get this one chance to break out
of a life that was suffocating her with poverty
and responsibility. But she didn't want to be indebted to that woman. She wanted for once in
her life for someone like Bunny to be indebted to
her . . . to be afraid of her . . . to listen to her
with respect.

By the eighth inning it was getting a bit chilly
and a slight drizzle began to fall. Dominic pulled
up the collar of his old tweed jacket; he never
wore a topcoat no matter what the weather, but
he should have brought a scarf. The chill and the
wet were making his arthritis act up. He wanted
some brandy, but all they sold in Bunsen Stadium was beer.

The fact was, he could no longer watch a complete game comfortably. Of course, he still loved
the game; it was his life. But of late, as his own
mortality had begun to press upon him with
greater and greater urgency, he wanted to utilize
what was left of his agility, of his mind, of his

imagination, for something else. He no longer
wanted to be only a part of baseball, however
beautiful and elegant it was in its conception and
execution. He had begun to walk a lot, outside
the city, to notice birds and reptiles and grasses
and insects and mushrooms. He had begun to
look at things with a different eye.

And there was another thing. As the years
passed his allegience to his old teammates, from
all the teams he had played on, had grown in
intensity—an allegience to the living and the
dead. But he found it very difficult to deal with
the new ballplayers. Something was always lost
in the translation. He knew it was foolish. Fifty
years ago or today—the moves, the strategy, the
techniques were still basically the same. They still
danced to the same tune—better now perhaps,
faster, stronger, but the difference, whatever it
was, did not explain his distancing himself from
this year's team. It was something else, and it
upset him because he didn't understand it. . . .
It upset him because he didn't understand why
he had absolutely no affection for any of the current players on the Oaktown Wolves.

It dawned on him that all these musings were
probably products of old age. He ran his hands
through his bristled hair, leaned forward, and
tried to concentrate on the game.

When the game was an out away from an
Oaktown victory, Bunny signaled that it was
time for them to start inching down toward the
dugout to extend their congratulations to Roger
and the team.

By the time they entered the dugout the last
out had been made, and it was a happy baseball
team and a happy management team sharing
congratulations in that strange atmosphere of
sweat and ribaldry which characterizes a win-
ner's locker room.

Someone handed Dominic a beer and he
moved to a far wall and sipped and listened to
all the opening-day nonsense. At least it was
warm there.

There was only one individual in the entire
locker room after the game who was not happy—
and that was the equipment manager, Moe Dallek.

He had good reason to be unhappy. It was a
long-standing tradition in Oaktown that if the
Wolves won on opening day, the winning pitcher
and the player who drove in the winning run
would autograph a whole box of baseballs which
would be distributed to the kids in the local ju-
venile detention home.

And now, when he needed them, he couldn't
locate a single one. The entire box of new baseballs he had set aside for the autograph party was
missing.

Then he realized that he must have left them
in the equipment locker that adjoined the visiting
dugout.

He looked around for someone to retrieve
them.

Alice Draught, one of the new ball girls, was
just about to leave with her father.

Moe called to her, apologizing to the father

silently with a shrug and a gesture, and hinting that it would only be a few minutes more.

He told Alice to go out through the dugout, onto the field, and check the equipment box just at the entrance to the visiting dugout.

He explained that he was missing a whole box of new balls.

"If it's not there, it's just lost," he said.

Alice ran through the dugout passage and onto the field. She was very happy. It had been the most exciting night of her life—all those people applauding whenever she had caught a ball, and cheering when she did one of her cartwheels.

The dark grass seemed to crunch beneath her feet as she made her way to the far dugout.

Virtually all the fans had already left the stadium, and the only lights remaining on were in center and right field where the cleanup crew had begun their work first because that was the area with, traditionally, the heaviest concentration of empty beer cans and other debris. It had always been the most raucous area of the stadium.

Alice saw the dull outline of the equipment box, lying low against the concrete wall of the dugout.

She bent over and fiddled with the latch.

She felt a sudden jolt of pain in her neck.

And then in her back.

She started to straighten up, and then she felt a jagged pain over her right shoulder—so severe that she screamed with every ounce of strength and resilience in her young body.

The scream died because something was gurgling in her mouth—filling her mouth.

She realized dimly it was her own blood, and she tried to turn, but everything seemed to be fading away.

As her life was sucked out of her there was a loathsome stench in her nostrils.

Her hand thrust back, groping desperately, and caught something wet and matted.

She fell onto the equipment box.

6

IT was one of the Oaktown detectives, Lambert, who had told Bunny and Dominic the truth when they arrived at the police station to discuss the beefing up of security at the stadium.

Until then they had believed what the newspapers and television station had reported: that seventeen-year-old Alice Draught, a ball girl for the Oaktown Wolves, had been raped and murdered in the opposing dugout after the conclusion of the opening game.

They had expected to be meeting Chief Tournier, but Lambert had said Tournier would join them shortly and ushered them into a small office.

Dominic leaned against the desk, noticing that the room was absolutely bare—no phone, no pencils, no nothing.

"The chief thinks you should know what is really going on," Lambert said. Bunny stared wide-eyed at Dominic; the detective's words were strange.

"About Alice Draught," he clarified.

Dominic looked at the detective: a short, squat man with thick brown hair and a brownish gray moustache. He didn't understand what more there could be to that horrible tragedy, and if there was more, what it could have to do with Bunny and himself.

"With Dr. Draught's permission we have withheld a great deal of information about the murder from the media."

"Like what?" Bunny asked, suddenly intrigued. After all, the murder had happened in her stadium.

"She wasn't raped. She was the victim of a perverse attack by either an animal or a lunatic. Her throat was ripped out. Other parts of her body that I won't mention in front of a lady were also ripped out. These parts were never found."

Dominic and Bunny stared at the man in uncomprehending horror as he carefully laid out the details, as if he were addressing a classroom.

Then Bunny buried her head in her hands. She remembered what Alice Draught had looked like—a vision of innocent, healthy perfection. A beautiful girl.

"In addition," the detective droned on, "there were very deep incisions across her back, and a small blood mark at the base of her neck, obviously made by the killer. He must have licked her with his tongue."

The door opened and Chief Tournier slipped

inside the room, closing the door quietly behind him. He saw by Dominic's and Bunny's expressions that Lambert was in the midst of his briefing, so he just waited and listened.

Tournier was wearing a loud black-and-white checked sports jacket, and he reminded Dominic of that poor dog, the Dalmation, who had gone crazy during the opening ceremony and died on the pavement from some kind of epileptic fit after he had savaged the police horse in the parade.

"We have to know all you can tell us about Julie Novick," Lambert said.

"About who?" Bunny asked, startled.

"Julie Novick, the mascot."

"What does she have to do with this? I don't know anything about her. She tried out. She was wonderful. She got the job."

Lambert explained: "She lost one of her wolf outfits just before the opening game, and she placed a notice on the bulletin board in the dugout to that effect. The claws and jaws of the wolf outfit could have done the kind of damage that was done to Alice Draught."

"Come on, Detective, are you saying—" Bunny responded, suddenly infuriated. She was cut off.

"Julie Novick," Lambert explained, "has an older brother named Matt who vanished right after the opening game. He had recently been released after serving a short sentence for sexually molesting a sixteen-year-old girl he met in a bowling alley. He offered to walk the girl home and then assaulted her in that small park on Boyle Street. The original charges against him were assault, attempted rape, and sodomy. He pleaded guilty to the molestation charge."

Bunny calmed down. "I didn't even know she had a brother," she replied, and then asked Dominic: "Did you?"

Dominic shook his head. He knew nothing at all about the Novick family.

Chief Tournier spoke for the first time: "We've checked out all the Portland players, all the grounds crew, everyone. Our only possibility right now is the kid, Matt. Maybe he used the wolf costume that his sister had lost."

Then he walked over to Bunny and placed his hand on her arm. "Miss Bunsen," he said softly, "I've been in this business a long, long time but I never saw anything like this. Never. The throat was ripped out of that girl's neck as if the killer were plucking a goddamn grape."

The chief motioned Detective Lambert to leave the room, and he did so.

"Something's terribly wrong," Chief Tournier said.

Bunny retreated quickly, wanting to get out of there: "We'll beef up security. We already have. People will be more watchful. You'll find that crazy kid, Chief."

The chief started to explain that he was talking about something else, that he was talking about the mutilation of the girl—but Bunny was already halfway out of the room, so his gaze fell on Dominic, who stared back.

"Do you know what I mean?" Tournier asked.

"We have a game tonight," Bunny called back

to Dominic. So Dominic didn't answer. The look
he had seen on the chief's face was incomprehen-
sible. It was fear—but fear of what?

Dominic followed Bunny out of the room
without saying a word.

He felt very tired and very old, and there was
a long evening ahead of him.

As he walked, the words of the detective
seemed to jump back into his consciousness . . .
throat torn out . . . parts missing . . . never
found.

Dominic had lived a long and sometimes violent life—in the army, in baseball, on the road.
He had seen men die and men get hurt. He had
seen injuries and blood. But he had never even
conceived of a crime where the entire throat was
ripped from a living person and then vanished.
And the rest? Oh God, he said, and realized he
had spoken out loud because Bunny had turned
and was staring at him, as if he were not well.

"I'm fine, I'm fine," he said, "just thinking
about that girl."

7

EVEN though by the fourth inning it was obvious that with any kind of luck the Oaktown Wolves were about to beat Portland for their first opening-series sweep in many years, the crowd was strangely subdued.

They had read about the murder-rape of the ball girl, and the substitute ball boy who had taken on Alice Draught's responsibilities seemed to make them uneasy.

Also, there was the unaccustomed sight of dozens of uniformed private security guards scattered throughout the stadium.

Bunny tried to keep her eyes away from Julie Novick in her wolf mascot outfit. It was too grotesque. That girl must be made of iron, she thought, to perform when she knows the police are searching for her brother and the missing wolf outfit.

But then Bunny remembered that the detective had said no one else knew that it was other than a murder-rape, which was bad enough. Not even Julie Novick knew the true horror of what had happened.

As the game wore on, Bunny grew more and more agitated remembering the police description of what had happened to Alice. There shouldn't be any baseball tonight, Bunny thought, perhaps never again.

She turned and stared at Dominic, who seemed intent on the game, and she realized suspension of the game would have been foolish—tragedies always occur, some more gruesome than others.

Dominic, in fact, was looking at the game but not with his usual intensity. His hands were curled tightly around the rail in front of him. The chill and the pain in his bones had been forgotten.

He heard sounds, he saw things, he was aware of Bunny alternately talking and being silent beside him.

But his mind was truly elsewhere, for he had, since he left the police station, remembered something.

Or rather, something the detective had told them rang something in his memory.

He did not know what—but the memory trace seemed to fester in his brain.

Was it something about the crime itself? Or about the girl?

He couldn't put his finger on it. As he had grown older these memory traces and lapses had, of course, become a prominent part of his life. He was always remembering that he had forgotten something. But this one was particularly vexing. It was as if he had forgotten an address; someone's address . . . or telephone number . . . It was as if he had forgotten something important.

Everything is so precarious, Bunny was thinking, everything is just a house of cards.

She had believed this was to be the season they won it all again. This was to be the season that her management and ownership and control of the Wolves would really bear fruit.

And now? Death in the night. Horrid, squalid, mutilating death in her ballpark. A girl who had never harmed anyone. A beautiful, good girl.

She sat back in her seat, her arms folded against the sudden chill, listening to the sounds of the game. She remembered how she had longed to come back to Oaktown and then summoned the courage to do so.

She remembered why she had decided to reassert her right to control the club . . . that sense she had of bringing the city together . . . of making the city whole . . . of using the team to rally everything that was good and decent in Oaktown. A romantic quest.

That was probably because she had grown to love baseball—it was one of those rare games where purity and style and beauty win.

Dominic brought his mind back to the game. He looked at the scoreboard. The Wolves were not very comfortably in front, 5-2.

Battaglia, the Wolves' second baseman, was on first with two out.

Dominic knew how Roger Randle managed. Battaglia would be going on the second pitch. The kid could steal bases; he was fast; he was quick; and above all he could read the pitchers.

The Portland manager figured Battaglia would be stealing on the first pitch. Portland pitched out. Battaglia wasn't going.

Dominic leaned forward, suddenly swept once again, for the millionth time in his long life, into the excitement and strategy surrounding a single pitch, a single runner, a single inning.

He could see the Portland catcher tensing, giving the signals.

They would not pitch out twice in a row. The pitcher stared Battaglia back and then stepped off the rubber.

The pitcher took the signals again and came in with a low, fast slider.

Battaglia was going. He beat the throw by a country mile.

Dominic grinned and sat back. He stared around as if to elicit the support of the other fans at a beautiful piece of baserunning. He turned back to the field to see whether the next batter would drive Battaglia in and give Oaktown a four-run lead.

A strong gust of wind crossed the field and the stands, sending papers and cups swirling about. Dominic didn't bend before the breeze. He felt it against his face; it was almost warm, and he felt then, in its wake, a fear that seemed to start at the base of his spine and twirl upward, like a snake.

He felt a sudden desire to flee, to get out of the stadium, to move his limbs, to walk.

He was sweating now. He leaned over, grasped Bunny's arm, and told her that he was weary, that he had to go home.

She smiled and said she understood. He moved toward the exit.

8

THREE men stood in the dank, empty room which constituted one area of the subbasement of Bunsen Stadium.

Along the far wall were old tarpaulins that had outlived their usefulness on the field. Along the side wall were shovels and picks and seed spreaders and assorted other tools of the groundskeeper's trade.

There was a single bulb burning overhead.

"I've been running all over the goddamn stadium looking for you," Dr. Draught said to Chief Tournier and Detective Lambert.

Lambert looked at his superior, waiting for him to answer; when he didn't, Lambert said: "We're moving around a bit. There are a lot of security forces to coordinate here tonight."

"You people are supposed to be cops, not coordinators," Dr. Draught yelled at them, and his voice echoed against the damp walls.

He caught his breath, straightened his shoulders, trying to restrain his anger. Then he asked: "What about Novick?"

"A positive ID was made on him in Marin County, California, only about five hours ago. We'll get him."

Tournier added: "We think he's heading for San Diego. He lived there briefly."

Draught retorted violently: "You think—that's all you people do—you damn think, and meanwhile that kid's making an ass of you. He's laughing at all of you."

The policemen stood silently, not responding. Lambert started to . . . but Tournier stopped him with a hand signal.

Alice Draught's father started to speak again, caught himself, then burst into sobs. His body wavered; he seemed to be falling.

Tournier and Lambert rushed over and helped him to one of the tarps, gently easing him down.

Between the massive sobs they could hear him: "Seventeen . . . she was only seventeen . . . her throat . . . her body violated . . . she was only seventeen years old . . . so beautiful . . . so—"

He buried his face in his hands. Tournier and Lambert stepped back and waited.

Dr. Draught regained control: "I'm sorry. Please forgive me. I'm sorry. I'll be better when you get him, when I can see that animal."

He stood up suddenly and tensed, as if testing his strength. He strode out the door without saying another word.

"That poor man," Tournier said.

"The kid, Matt Novick, is moving fast. Do you think he has a car?"

"Probably. But it doesn't matter."

"We don't have a make on the car."

"I mean," Tournier said gently, "that I don't really believe Matt Novick is guilty of murdering and mutilating Alice Draught."

Lambert raised his eyebrows at the chief's words. Tournier rarely made such deliberate statements on these matters. He waited and watched.

"He's all we got," Lambert noted.

Tournier sat down on the tarp and looked kindly at his associate, of whom he was genuinely fond.

"It would take someone with enormous strength, no matter the instrument he used, to do that to a living human being. And as sad and as horrible as the truth is, we know that the girl was mutilated while still alive; that she died from shock and bleeding as a consequence of the mutilations."

"Then who? Or what? A wolf? A bear? That's crazy. I mean this happened in a city ballpark."

"No. No animal either. Remember what the medical examiner said; he found no trace of animal hairs, no trace of saliva, no trace of animal blood."

"Then that leaves a strong man, a giant, a man with some kind of totally abnormal strength—perhaps psychotic, perhaps on speed," Lambert responded.

"I don't know."

"Well, it has to be that, then," Lambert pressed. Tournier's hesitation, his look, his speech was making the younger man uncomfortable.

"Maybe," Tournier finally said.

"You're thinking something else, Chief, I can tell."

Tournier said: "Why don't you take a walk around and see what's happening. I'll be here."

Lambert knew he had been dismissed, and he left without saying another word. Tournier found the cold coffee he had started an hour ago and lit a cigarette while he sipped it. He rarely smoked cigarettes anymore.

Only once before had a crime affected him so badly, and that was years ago when he had first started out in police work in a small Illinois town.

It was that crime, so many years ago, that constantly intruded in his imagination now; that made him feel he was now facing something he could neither deal with nor comprehend.

In that Illinois town, there was a community of Moravians; devout people who farmed without machinery and who kept to themselves.

A young Moravian woman had been murdered and mutilated. It had been particularly gruesome. The head literally had been chewed off and one hand and one foot.

A week later the body of a young man had been dumped in front of the police station. There were two bullet holes in his forehead. Pinned to his chest, through the flesh, was a note saying the crime had been solved, that this young man had killed the woman.

The note was long and rambling, speckled with blood, and Tournier had always remembered a few words the unknown vigilante had used in the note. It said that the young man had been mentally ill, and Tournier could confirm this diagnosis by studying the corpse, which would show that the murderer had been "afflicted with a devil's spleen that had sucked from him all knowledge of good."

These words were so strange and so absurd— as if they had been lifted from an ancient text— that Tournier had never forgotten them.

He finished the coffee and flung the empty container against the far wall, suddenly furious at himself for having lapsed into a kind of romantic nonsense.

He ground out the cigarette, determined to concentrate on what the department had—and they had a suspect, Matt Novick—along with an MO, a wolf suit with very powerful artificial claws and teeth.

It was entirely possible that the kid had an accomplice and that their combined strengths had enabled them to pursue and accomplish their gruesome actions under the influence of booze or maybe some kind of hallucinogen. He resolved to proceed only along those lines until something else concrete happened. His vague feelings were both irrelevant and harmful to the investigation.

9

DOMINIC walked randomly when he left the stadium, until he grew weary. Then he looked for a bar or a coffee shop or just someplace to sit.

He was in that section of the city called the Armory District because during World War II a National Guard unit had briefly been stationed there. Now there were streets of two-story town houses and a thriving shopping center.

The streets were deserted. Oaktown was a car city; people really didn't walk unless they had to or they were marching in a parade.

Something flickered off to one side. He grinned to himself. A lifetime in the minor leagues had made him immediately sensitive to a blinking light, because in the towns and cities he had played in all his life, a blinking light meant only one of two things—a cop car or a bar, usually the latter.

The current furor over drugs in sports only amused Dominic. When he was playing, on any given day, half the team would be drunk, and the other half drying out.

It was a small bar, tucked away behind a dry-cleaning store. He remembered going in there years ago when he was still drinking seriously. It was amazing it had survived all the redevelopment around it.

It smelled good inside—sweet and sour—and there was a long, low murmur in the air, like people were whispering about something important.

He went to the center of the bar and sat on a stool. It was a long bar and about fifteen men were scattered along it, some singly and some in groups.

He relaxed. It was dark enough so that no one would recognize him and start one of those interminable baseball conversations about the Wolves' chances this year and why they had collapsed last year. Dominic loved talking baseball, but only if the conversation was about the machinery of the game—not won-lost ratios.

He ordered a brandy and a stein of ale and slowly drifted into the softness of it all . . . feeling the brandy warm him . . . tasting and rolling on his tongue the slightly bitter mix of ale and brandy.

"Coach."

He heard someone call him, and it broke him out of his reverie; but then he thought that he must have fallen asleep and it was a dream.

But then it came again—low, desperate: "Coach."

And Dominic swung on his stool, toward the sound, and found himself staring at Jackie Cannon.

Dominic sat back, revulsed by the sight; Jackie looked even worse now than when he had seen him, confused and frightened, in the ladies' room at Victor's; when Bunny thought she had been attacked by him. His face was still bruised from Roger's fist.

The man's whole body seemed to be withering; his clothes were filthy; and one eye was closed as if he had suffered a stroke.

Dominic realized the man he was looking at was only about fifty years old—he looked eighty.

And there in his hand were those stupid Indian shells that he had always carried when he was playing—a sort of rosary.

Dominic's initial horror was swiftly lessened by nostalgia—by the memory of how good a player Jackie Cannon had been. It was Jackie Cannon who had made the 1963 champions into a juggernaut when everyone had counted them out.

He remembered the man's hustle, his sense of camaraderie, the way he had studied every pitcher, every batter, every manager—how he could pick up things that no one else ever saw.

"Help me out, Coach," begged this derelict apparition of a ballplayer.

Suddenly the bartender intervened, coming up near where Dominic was sitting and saying to Jackie Cannon: "Get the hell out of here. I told you yesterday, don't come in again or you're going to fly out on your ass."

Dominic said, quickly and quietly: "Thanks, but he's not bothering me. Give him a blackberry brandy and then he'll go."

The bartender stared at Dominic as if he were crazy; as if he didn't know what he was getting into by buying the man a drink—but he poured the drink and shoved it under Jackie Cannon's nose.

Jackie struggled to climb on the stool next to Dominic; finally he made it.

"Been a long time, Coach," he whispered.

Dominic stared at him, startled, and then realized that Jackie probably didn't remember the incident with Bunny. He probably couldn't remember anything that happened longer than twelve minutes ago.

He leaned closer to Dominic and his smell nauseated the older man who, however, out of politeness, did not move away.

"I never could hit the long ball. You never liked me because of that, Coach, huh? You loved the long ball."

And then Jackie drank the blackberry brandy, sweetish and thick, in one long gulp.

"Help me out again, Coach," he begged, and Dominic told the bartender to refill the glass.

"I been ailing, Coach. Could use old Doc Draught to get me going."

The name "Draught" coming from the derelict's mouth confused Dominic. Was Jackie Cannon talking about the father of the girl who had been killed? Then he remembered that the trainer on the 1963 team had been named Doc Draught.

He had forgotten all about him. God, Dominic thought, that must have been Alice Draught's grandfather. Dominic had always disliked him because he kept strewing rolls of tape and bandages all over the clubhouse.

He sat back, sure he now remembered old Doc Draught, who hadn't in fact been so old then, but had crawled about like a goddamn turtle.

Dominic ordered another drink for himself and another for Jackie Cannon. He wondered if the game was over already, and if it was, who had won. The Wolves had been ahead, but it's not over till it's over.

They sat together in silence and drank.

Dominic knew he had drunk too much already because he was beginning to feel light and warm; he was beginning to feel that he and the derelict were part of a team. It was that feeling which he missed most from his playing days, that slow unwinding after a tough game, that unspoken companionship of grown men earning their bread from a very unpredictable game.

Finally, he said, grinning into his ale: "God, Jackie, that was a year, wasn't it? Nineteen sixty-three."

The grin became a hearty laugh and he added: "Now here we are. The 1963 Manager of the Year in the Pacific Coast League and the 1963 Most Valuable Player."

He turned to the derelict.

Jackie Cannon was not laughing. He was playing with his shells with one hand and the other hand held his drink tightly.

"What's the matter, Jackie, booze got your brain? You don't remember?" Dominic asked, hurt by the derelict's lack of response.

"Remember what?"

"Nineteen sixty-three."

"What happened in 1963?" Jackie mocked.

"The championship. We won it all. All. All of it, Jackie, you, me, and all the others, together."

Jackie finished his drink.

"Fool," he said to Dominic.

"Who's a fool, you pathetic wino?" Dominic yelled, his fury fueled by the brandy.

Suddenly Jackie Cannon slid off the stool and moved away, facing Dominic, his arm extended toward the old man in a sort of threat, a sort of accusation.

"We won nothing in 1963," the derelict screamed, and then turned to the others at the bar and repeated his words again.

The bartender came from behind the bar and grabbed Jackie Cannon by the shoulders. The derelict fought back but was no match and was dragged foot by foot to the front door, screaming obscenities at Dominic and everyone else.

Then he stopped resisting. The bartender released his hold. Dominic could see him trying to catch his breath. He was trying to say something else to Dominic.

Dominic moved toward him. Jackie Cannon was weeping now. The bartender moved away, anxious to let the derelict leave without any more violence.

"We won death, Coach. We won death in

nineteen-sixty-three," Jackie Cannon said, and staggered and fell, slamming his face against the floor.

The bartender moved toward him again, but this time Dominic got there first, and tenderly helped the man who used to play for him rise up.

He half carried Jackie Cannon into the drizzling night. Once outside, the derelict shook him off and started to walk away.

Then he turned, unsteadily, and raised one hand in salutation.

Dominic smiled at him and mimicked the gesture.

"We didn't win in 1963, Coach. We bought it. And now we're paying for it."

The words had come out of Jackie Cannon's mouth slowly, with great effort.

And Dominic heard every startling syllable.

He watched Jackie Cannon walk away with that odd gait that alcoholics use, like fat sailors.

Dominic did not go back into the bar. Jackie's words, his charge, his confusing description, his crazy perspective, had touched something inside him—something he could not articulate but had always felt, something about 1963 that he could never explain.

He stood for the longest time where he was, oblivious to everything. He felt that everything he knew and believed in was being sucked out of the world.

10

"**Y**OU going with us for the three games in Las Vegas?"

"I'm the owner, you fool. I go everywhere."

Tim Shea laughed at Bunny Bunsen's response. He laughed because he often forgot that she was, in fact, the owner, and with a snap of the fingers could dispense with him as a ballplayer and as a lover.

He secretly believed that it was Bunny who had persuaded Roger to renew his contract this year, because his rookie year in the PCL, last year, after two years in Class B ball, had been disastrous: a 6.2 earned-run average working out of the bullpen.

He turned over on the bed and cradled her head against his chest.

Bunny felt good lying there. Their lovemaking was, as usual, wonderful. For a silly young farm kid he was amazingly sophisticated and intense . . . above all, intense.

They had been lovers for more than a year, using a small house on the outskirts of the city that belonged to but was never inhabited by one of her closest childhood friends—now in Chicago.

Bunny knew all about the rumors that kept swirling, about how she slept with ballplayers. It was partially true—however, she slept with a ballplayer, singular, one at a time.

Perhaps, she realized, it was her affection for men like Tim Shea that had brought her back to Oaktown to take control of the team, and not the other reasons, most of them philosophical, she had always used to justify her actions.

The moment she had laid eyes on Tim Shea she wanted him, and knew he wanted her.

It was odd; she was only about two years older than he was, but she sometimes felt twenty years older. She felt from the very start that he was almost her kid brother—a bit wild, a bit fanciful. But her erotic feeling for him was surely not brotherly.

They were so strange, all the young ballplayers, so outside the norm of young men she had known in the past.

For them, baseball was a magical world, the sum total of their experience and dreams. They talked about the world as if it were a joke, and they talked about baseball as if it contained all the wisdom, beauty, and challenge they could ever want.

"I think crazy Larrabee is beginning to suspect," Tim said.

"Suspect what?"

"About us."

"Well, he's your friend, so he must have gotten it from you."

"Why would I tell him anything? You know, everyone thinks Larrabee is just crazy, but he's also very smart."

"Too bad he never learned how to hit," she said, teasing him, knowing that Tim disliked anyone to speak poorly of Larrabee, who was the team clown, who was always engaged in a series of on-the-field and off-the-field practical jokes. The problem was, it was doubtful that Larrabee would see much action this season unless someone got hurt.

She realized she should start exercising more tact when evaluating the talents of ballplayers. They were very sensitive to criticism, like children. But it had been hard to be tactful recently because she had felt a growing sense of power, of strength, as if she could control events just by willing a thing to happen. It was very odd—as if there were now another dimension to her understanding of the game, even to her consciousness.

Bunny ran her hand up Tim's well-muscled chest and along his neck. She twisted around, took his hand, and placed it over her breast, holding it there, musing, quiet, relaxed. A single light across the room sent some flickering shadows over her legs.

Suddenly Tim laughed.

"What's so funny?" she asked.

"Larrabee. The other day he wondered if you were going to apply for the ball girl job."

She pushed him away violently.

"What the hell is the matter with you?" he demanded.

"I don't appreciate that kind of sick humor. It was a horrible thing."

"Well, that's Larrabee, a bit weird. Hell, he's just as sorry about the girl as anyone else. And if there was a posse, like in the Old West, to hunt down the maniac who did it—Larrabee would be the first to sign up."

She leaned forward and clasped her arms around her legs. Her nakedness had suddenly made her feel vulnerable. She stared at Tim Shea, who now lay there with his eyes closed, tired, almost indolent. She realized he didn't know the real extent of the crime. He thought it was a murder-rape. He didn't know about the mutilations; he didn't know anything.

She sat there huddled in a ball, remembering the hideous things the detective had told her.

"Tim," she said softly.

"Yeah?" He opened his eyes and raised his head a bit.

"Nothing," she said, and moved over to his side and held him tightly, thinking of the girl, and what the girl must have felt before blessed unconsciousness came—the pain, the horror.

Then she wondered where Dominic had gone—it was so unlike him to walk out before a game was finished. He had seemed uneasy, as if he were about to be ill. He probably went to a bar, she thought, and had a few brandies, and then went home to sleep.

She realized she should stop acting like his daughter, like one of those daughters who are overly protective of their fathers, making them seem more feeble than they really are. But the fact was—Dominic was the only real connection she had with her father, a thin, tenuous line going back to 1963 and before. And she knew the truth—that her father had been a sonofabitch— and she knew that Dominic now sugar-coated all the memories because he thought it disrespectful to the dead to tell the truth about them if that truth was less than nice.

Maybe this year, she mused, as she lay entwined with the young relief pitcher; maybe this year they would repeat the miracle of 1963, and then, she felt, something about the memory of her father would change—she would be able to retrieve his face and thoughts.

She felt Tim Shea beginning to stir again.

11

AFTER sweeping Portland in the opening series, the Oaktown Wolves got blown out in their opener at Las Vegas. The players were not too depressed, because they had to take a loss sooner or later and besides, this was Vegas, and all the teams in the PCL loved playing there for obvious reasons, not least of which was the excellent accommodations. Gambling resort hotels traditionally charge low room rates in order to entice visitors, thus allowing the PCL teams to stay at a hotel utterly different from their usually dreary second-class motel.

"I'm not putting in a curfew, but use your common sense," Roger said as the team dressed. His comments were greeted with good-natured hoots.

Larrabee sidled up to the manager and whispered in his ear: "I guarantee you big winnings tonight, Rog. I'm talking about a hundred thou. All I need is a little stake."

"Get away from me, Larrabee," Roger shouted. "You can't even count, so how the hell are you going to win at blackjack."

"The pictures, I look at the pictures," Larrabee said. Then he looked around for his friend Tim Shea, who was still sitting in a corner, dejected.

"What the hell," Larrabee said to his friend, "they only got three extra-base hits off you, Champ; I mean you showed them who's boss."

The shoe from Shea whistled past Larrabee's ear and slammed into the tin locker.

To hell with him, Larrabee thought, and he circulated throughout the locker room, displaying the hundred and fifty dollars he had and looking for a partner to match the money so he could gamble with someone. There were no takers. They all loved Larrabee because he was funny, but they didn't want to drink or gamble with him; he was too frenetic, too crazy, you never knew what he was going to do.

To hell with all of them, Larrabee concluded, finished dressing, and walked out. He was wearing a red jacket, a black and white shirt, and well-worn jeans over an elaborate and custommade pair of boots.

He didn't look like a ballplayer, like his friend Shea—he looked like a tubercular cowboy; very tall, very skinny, and very bent. He was almost bald, with a fringe of dark hair around the sides, a prominent nose, and high jutting cheekbones.

Not the big casinos, he reasoned, but downtown. And there he walked, having his first drink

on the floor at Circus Circus; a vodka martini
with a twist. He lost a hundred bucks at the
blackjack table in about fifteen minutes. His system had obviously not worked too well, although
he thought it would have been different if he'd
had a real stake so he wouldn't have to play
scared.

That left him with a little less than fifty dollars, so he husbanded it carefully, going from bar
to bar in the downtown area, drinking just beer,
listening to the music, watching the women. He
knew he was drinking a bit too much, because
he was getting morose; he was beginning to think
about another season on the bench. He started to
curse Roger Randle and the whole Oaktown
management under his breath; he started to think
about quitting and going to Canada; he started
to think of ways he could pick up his hitting—of
what he was doing wrong, of what he had always done wrong. Hell, he would never be able
to hit for the distance, but he could put wood on
the ball . . . he could make contact.

By one in the morning he was beginning to
have delusions that he was in the majors, playing
left field for the Cincinnati Reds and making
locker-room jokes with Dave Parker.

He could visualize himself in the Reds' uniform
with the big *C* plastered on his shirt; he could
see himself digging in carefully against Dwight
Gooden of the Mets. He could feel himself bunt-
ing against Scott of the Astros, breaking up his
no-hitter with a brilliantly laid down bunt, just
dropping it in the pocket on the first-base side.

He could see himself charging the mound after Valenzuela of the Dodgers had winged him with a fastball.

Larrabee walked out of a bar called Dollar Bills at two in the morning, and he just stood on the street, a bit unsteady, realizing he hadn't the slightest notion which way the hotel was.

He did remember that the hotel was on a wide boulevard, so he started walking toward an intersection he dimly perceived in the distance. His stomach was acting up now and he was a bit dizzy. He searched in his pockets for some sucking candy or gum, but he had none left.

The longer he walked the more the intersection and its lights seemed to recede in the distance. He spotted a brightly lit all-night coffee shop and leaned against the window for a while until one of the waitresses started knocking against the pane that he should move on. Larrabee made an obscene gesture to her, but he did move; he turned the corner into a clean alley lined with wooden crates and dumpsters.

He unzipped his pants and urinated against the side of a dumpster.

Suddenly he felt unable to breathe. His mouth fell open trying to swallow air.

He tried to walk, but he couldn't move. He tried to zip up his pants, but he had no strength.

Then he realized he was in the grip of someone; that two arms were wrapped around his chest from behind, constricting his breathing, imprisoning his own arms.

At the end of the arms something glinted. No,

these are not arms around me, he thought. They're covered with filthy matted hair.

He started to scream, but there was no breath.

He tried to push his arms outward, to release the grip of whatever was wrapped around him. But the things would not move.

Eyes bulging, mouth open in silent screams, muscles taut with panic—he tried to fight what seemed to be crushing the life from his body.

From behind him, he heard sounds. His nostrils dilated at a smell so putrid and musky that he gagged on his own tongue.

And then he heard another sound—the sound of his own body ripping.

The pain came at the exact moment he could see the clothes and flesh and bone of his stomach opening.

The last thing he saw was his own liver.

12

THEY followed the police officer down the long, narrow corridor. The tiles of the walls were spotless. The floor had been freshly mopped. They entered a chamber lined with body lockers. The officer led them along the rows of lockers, which seemed to be arranged alphabetically by name. He stopped and slid out a locker.

Bunny and Dominic stared down at Larrabee's distinctive face, made more distinctive by death.

"Where's Roger?" Dominic asked.

"He's waiting for my call at the hotel."

"Call him," Dominic said. "Tell him Larrabee's dead; tell everyone who has to know."

Bunny nodded, quickly kissing Dominic on the cheek, and was gone. Dominic heard her heels clicking against the polished hallway floor.

He looked again at the young ballplayer. He remembered what that drunken bum Jackie Cannon had told him in the bar; that the only thing they had won in 1963 was death. Was it

Larrabee's death they had won, or the girl's? Whose death, where?

"What happened?" Dominic asked the police officer.

The officer pulled the sheet all the way back.

Dominic grew dizzy and almost fell; the strong arm of the cop came to his support.

Larrabee's stomach had been ripped open and the contents removed. There was little left inside.

"It wasn't the medical examiner who did that," the cop noted, "it was the murderer. His insides were gone."

Dominic stared in horror at the cop. "What do you mean, his insides?"

"Liver, kidney, heart, lungs, intestines—the man's viscera were gone. He was emptied out, like someone took a spoon and scooped him out."

"That's Larrabee, Eric Larrabee," Dominic muttered, trying to distance himself from the description.

"Are you sure?"

"I am sure," Dominic said.

"That kid is really freaky."

"What kid?"

"We spoke to Chief Tournier in Oaktown. He told us about Matt Novick. About how he's a suspect in the murder of a young girl. He uses a wolf costume he stole from his sister who's the mascot for the baseball team. That kid must be superman. But we heard he robbed a fast-food place in Reno and is heading this way. He probably passed through already, on his way out. The

trouble is, he hooked up with two other lunatics.
We have a positive ID on one of them—a biker
named Rowse with about ten warrants outstand-
ing. The third character we have no positive ID
for—all we know is that he appears to be His-
panic."

Dominic reached out a hand to the corpse, but
he didn't touch it.

"What is that?" he asked, pointing to massive
bruises around the corpse's midsection.

"It looks as if he was almost crushed to death
from behind before they ripped out his stomach.
I hope he was unconscious by then," said the cop
as he turned the body on its side, revealing more
bruises.

"When did you find him?"

"About four in the morning. We traced his
moves as best we could. He lost some money at
Circus Circus and then he started hitting downtown bars. He was drunk at the end; his BAL
went through the roof."

Who gives a goddamn about his blood alcohol
level, Dominic thought. He felt a desire to stroke
the young man, to somehow convey his horror
and compassion, but it was all too late, much too
late. Jackie Cannon had said the Wolves had won
death in 1963. These words weighed more heavily on him now. What did they mean? Why was
all this happening? Who was that kid, Matt Novick, wandering the empty spaces with his grotesque mission, now adding bikers, crazies, and
God knows who else?

"Do you know his people?" the cop asked.

Dominic was at first startled by the question: it was such an old-fashioned expression—his people.

"No," said Dominic, and then realized that he didn't even know where Larrabee was born, where he came from, what he thought about. All Dominic knew about Larrabee was that he was good field/no hit and the team's clown, and was always getting in some kind of trouble. He had liked Larrabee, but everyone did.

They hovered there, the cop and the old ballplayer, staring down at what they saw, as if leaving that mutilated body would be somehow sacrilegious; as if only by standing beside the corpse could the great gap in his stomach be filled; as if only by their presence could they somehow bring back his vital organs.

"So fucking grotesque," the cop said.

"Did you search for it?"

"What do you mean?"

"I mean his stuff, his organs. Did you look around?"

"Of course. We looked for anything and everything. We found nothing. No weapons. No clues. No witnesses. No liver. No kidney. No nothing."

Dominic realized the absurdity of his questions. But he didn't know what else to ask. He felt he had to do something. He felt he had to ask. He wanted Jackie Cannon to be with him now, to stare at the body, to say once again what he had said in the ugly bar: "All you won was death."

What he finally did ask was: "How do we go about picking up the body?"

"Just fill out a form upstairs," said the cop.

Dominic followed the cop back along the spotless halls and into the office. He filled out all the required forms.

Ten minutes later he was out on the street in the brilliant Vegas sun. He started to walk toward the hotel where Bunny and the team would be waiting for him. He walked very slowly, keeping to the curbside, not sure of himself; not sure of his gait; not sure of his ability to assimilate what he had seen.

Two men were walking toward him; he moved away quickly, afraid.

And then, a mother and two children came up behind him; he gave them a wide berth. He wanted, above all, right then to avoid any human contact.

That strange memory of something he could not bring forth started to bother him again; that sense of seeing something or hearing something that was very important.

He stopped by a bench, stared at it for a while, and then sat down. He stared at the traffic: new-model cars, buses, campers, beat-up trucks. Matt Novick and his murderous companions could be in one of them. He didn't know what Matt Novick looked like. He couldn't even remember what his sister looked like, even though he had sat on the panel that judged her wolf the best mascot for Oaktown.

He closed his eyes and listened. The sounds

were jarring: horns, brakes, shuffles, calls. Vegas was a twenty-four-hour town.

He could see Larrabee's face, eyes closed, on the morgue slab. He could see the cop stripping down the sheet and displaying the horror of his body.

He started to get up but felt a pain in his shoulder, so he sat back down again and began to massage the offended part. The pain slowly vanished. He was astonished at the strength he still had in his broken fingers.

The sound of screeching brakes cut through the morning sun. A low-slung red car had missed a yellow light and was trying to stop. It finally did, but swerved halfway around in the attempt, tying up traffic in the other lane. No one was hurt.

Dominic stared at the red car. His memory seemed to open up, suddenly, as suddenly as the car had braked.

He remembered what he had forgotten and what he had just seen again without even taking notice.

Both the girl who had been murdered in Oaktown and Larrabee had had a small red mark on the back and base of the neck. It had been so insignificant to the Las Vegas cop that he hadn't even mentioned it.

Dominic remembered what the detective had told him in Oaktown—that the mark seemed to have been made by the maniac, who had licked the victim with a bloody tongue.

The memory was shattering. He had entirely

forgotten about it because it had happened years ago. About a quarter of a century ago.

Walter Bunsen had come into the locker room, just as they had started their memorable run for the championship in 1963.

He had laughingly said that his shoeshine boy had told him they would win the Pacific Coast League title if just three of the players put a little blood on the bases of their necks; some good old-fashioned war paint.

And Walter had said, laughingly, that he just came from the butcher with enough to dab the whole team. Three would do—but the more the merrier.

Come and get it, he had said. It was just one of the hundreds of crazy things that happened during that miraculous year; everybody was talking and acting crazy.

Dominic tried to remember which players had daubed themselves. He couldn't remember, but it didn't matter.

They had put the blood on the exact spot where the killer had marked Alice Draught and Larrabee.

Now what Jackie Cannon had said . . . now his drunken words were like an open wound. He realized he had to keep all this to himself, until he got back to Oaktown—until he could talk to Chief Tournier.

13

THE Oaktown Wolves split the four-game series in Las Vegas, and they returned home after the first week of the season with a 5 and 2 record, good enough to give them first place in the Northern Division of the PCL.

But they didn't go home to a parade. They went home for a funeral—Larrabee's; and they went home to a city in shock.

The funeral was grim. Thousands of ordinary citizens showed up, blocking approaches to the cemetery. One newspaper concentrated on the bad luck involved, how two persons associated with the team had been brutally murdered—and how it could have been any other two persons.

Another newspaper concentrated on the personality of the suspect—Matt Novick—dragging out his sexual molestation convictions, speculation over why he might have killed both the ball girl and the ballplayer—and gave his case to an academic psychologist who further speculated on his morbid and pathological personality.

But there were other views expressed—on the street, in the bars, in the schools.

Information was beginning to leak . . . people were slowly beginning to hear strange stories . . . bits and pieces of what might have really transpired . . . of horrible mutilations. Few people really believed the speculations, which grew more and more bizarre. What was real and credible was the fear that now seemed to radiate out from the very center of the stadium and touch everyone. People moved a little more quickly, spoke a little more softly, kept their eyes open when formerly they would shut them and nap.

Tournier sat in the booth of the coffee shop that was situated next to Oaktown's largest auto dealer. It was mid-morning. The breakfast crowd had gone and the lunch crowd had not yet arrived. Out of habit, the chief evaluated the customers and their positions, then let his eyes wander toward the kitchen, the bathrooms, and out the window on the side that gave a full view of the auto dealer's showroom. It was the habit of a longtime careful cop and Tournier was surely that. His eyes moved to the front window and he saw Lambert waiting in the car. Lambert had driven him here and Lambert would wait until he was through. Chief Tournier was not one for the trappings of rank, but he dearly loved and appreciated the luxury of having a detective first class to chauffeur him around. And anyway,

Tournier was, by his own admission, a lousy driver.

Then Dominic walked inside, looked around, spotted the chief, and walked over.

Tournier could see he was in some kind of pain—he gimped—probably arthritic, Tournier thought, like all old ballplayers.

Dominic nodded greetings and slid into the booth opposite him.

"Want anything?" Tournier asked.

"Coffee."

Tournier ordered a cup of coffee for the older man and asked for a refill for himself.

"Thanks for coming," Dominic said. Tournier nodded in response. Dominic carefully stirred some sugar into the coffee and then some milk. He sipped it. He sat back.

"I identified Larrabee's body in Las Vegas," he said.

"So I heard."

"He had a red mark on the base of his neck—a small one—just like Alice Draught."

"So I heard."

"In 1963, a few of our players put the same blood mark on them—good luck war paint."

Tournier stared at him; he didn't know what the hell Dominic was talking about.

"Only, of course, it was cow's blood, or pig's blood, or something like that."

"Why did they do it?"

"It's like not changing your socks on a winning streak. It was the brainchild of Walter Bunsen, and what he said went. I think a kid who shined his shoes had had a dream that the Wolves would win the championship if they daubed themselves."

"Okay."

"I mean, isn't it funny that twenty-five years later that mark would show itself again—only this time on two murdered and mutilated people?"

"It's a coincidence."

Dominic stared at Tournier quickly, angrily, and then lowered his stare. He knew the police chief was with him . . . was even more frightened than he was . . . but he also realized that the man would maintain his professional mask.

Dominic continued: "Before we left for Vegas I met an old ballplayer from the 1963 team."

"Who?"

"Jackie Cannon."

"I don't know him."

"He's a drunk, a half-Indian drunk. Your wagon probably picked him up ten times last year."

"What does he have to do with this?"

"He told me the 1963 championship was bought."

"Bought? By whom?"

"I don't know."

"What else did he tell you?"

Dominic didn't answer for a while. He shifted uncomfortably in his seat, and his eyes roamed around the coffee shop seeking familiar faces; but no one there was familiar.

"He said, 'The only thing we won in 1963 was death.'"

Tournier laughed nervously: "And you thought you had won the PCL championship."

"Right."

"And now you think you really won Alice Draught's and Larrabee's deaths?"

Tournier's words were exactly what he had been thinking but could not articulate.

"Jackie said we won death."

"What you're thinking is outside the realm of police work," Tournier said.

"What I *saw* is outside the realm of police work," Dominic retorted.

"Like what?"

"Like a stomach emptied of its contents, ripped out. Like a girl surgically mutilated by someone who can't be identified."

"We have a suspect," Tournier reminded him.

"The last time I saw you, after the Draught murder, you told me that something was terribly wrong . . . that you were faced with something you couldn't explain."

"Okay. You made your point."

"You don't really believe that kid did all this?" Dominic pressed. He needed an ally.

"No, I don't."

"Then who?"

"Or what?" Tournier countered. He bent forward and folded his hands. They stared at each other. They felt the connection between them. They knew that each knew something, felt something, that could not be spoken about to anyone else.

"I don't know what Jackie Cannon meant when he said we won death," Dominic blurted out. "I don't know who bought the championship and from whom. I don't know if anything he said has anything to do with what is happening now. But I feel that something terrible is happening, because no one understands. That frightens me. Very much. I'm old, Chief, and I'm very scared."

They heard a tapping on the window. It was Lambert, gently knocking his ring at the window for his chief's attention.

"Excuse me for a minute," Tournier said, sliding out from the booth and walking toward the window. Lambert had written something on notepaper and pressed it against the pane. "Some trouble at Cathedral."

Tournier nodded, waved his hand at the detective signifying that he should check it out, and then returned to the booth.

"Some trouble at the parochial school," Tournier explained to Dominic.

Dominic blurted out his words again: "What I want to say is . . . why I wanted to meet you here—" He stopped suddenly, in mid-sentence, not sure how to continue. He ran one gnarled hand through his bristled, short gray hair.

Tournier waited, his fingers fiddling with his now empty coffee cup.

"I have something to do with the murders."

It was an astonishing comment. Tournier
didn't quite know how to reply.

"How?"

"Something in the past."

"Be specific."

"I can't be specific."

"Do you mean you wish me to consider you as
an accessory to murder?"

"Of course not."

"Then tell me what you mean. I came here. I
want to hear it."

"All this horror and blood is a payback."

"For what?"

"I don't know."

Tournier signaled to the waitress for more coffee; she arrived and poured reluctantly. It was
past the breakfast hour, when second cups of coffee were given free, but she would be uncomfortable about charging the police chief and the
much revered "Coach" for a second cup. Yet her
boss required her to charge. She compromised by
only refilling the cups halfway. Tournier arched
his eyebrows at her but said nothing.

Dominic sipped the fresh coffee.

"I'm an old man," he said, "and I've played a
kid's game all my life. But I'm not stupid."

"No one ever said you were."

"I don't believe in God. I don't believe in the
Devil. I believe in chance. And I believe in another world."

"Another world?"

"Something we don't see. That sometimes
breaks through."

"Are you telling me that something from this other world destroyed those two people?"

"Maybe. Or something that people used to call beasts."

"A beast?" Tournier guffawed quietly. "You mean a hopped-up kid dressed in a wolf outfit?"

"No."

"You mean a bear, a wolf, a slavering, crazed, rabid beast who slunk down somehow from its lair in the Coast Range?"

"No."

"Then explain yourself, goddammit," Tournier said, "explain yourself."

"Not human, Chief, it can't be human. Not animal, Chief, it can't be animal."

"A spirit made flesh?" Tournier asked.

"You're making fun of me now."

"No, Dominic, if I can call you Dominic. I'm not making fun of you. I'm trying to get you to help me."

Dominic pressed on to defend his beliefs. He interrogated: "Why mutilate, then, if it was not what I think it was?"

"Because the killer is sick."

"Why have the organs vanished?"

"Maybe the killer is sexually attracted to them. Maybe he keeps them in a plastic bag and takes them out only to masturbate over them."

The imagery sickened Dominic, and he fought back an impulse to vomit. He gagged. He hiccupped. He got control.

"And why the red mark?"

"A kiss. Psychotic killers love their victims."

"How can a human exhibit that kind of strength?"

"I once saw a cripple send five cops to the hospital when he was in a psychotic rage. One of the cops died."

"But both victims had something to do with the team."

"Coincidence again."

"It's more than that. The girl was a ball girl. Her grandfather was the trainer on the 1963 team."

"Hell, Dominic, in this town, every other person is related to someone who once had something to do with the team."

Dominic persisted: "No clues left; no hair; no fingerprints; no nails, no nothing on the bodies."

"Not true," Tournier said. "The killer left bruises on Larrabee. And the blood mark on the neck of the girl showed two blood types—A and O. The girl was A. Larrabee's mark showed only O. So whoever killed and mutilated both had blood type O, whether or not it was the same person. Matt Novick, by the way, is O—but then again, O is the most common blood type. It was the power and precision of the mutilations that prevented significant clues. Our psychotic is not sloppy. But if the same individual murdered them both, he is getting a bit sloppier. Witness the bruises on Larrabee."

"I'm not making myself clear. You don't understand me."

"Dominic, I was raised by a superstitious

French-Canadian grandmother in a small town in Quebec. I understand you."

"What the hell does that have to do with anything?"

"She once caught me masturbating. She told me if I ever did that again I would become like Monsieur Garnier."

"Who is Garnier?"

"I'll tell you some other time," Tournier said.

Dominic didn't care. The conversation had exhausted him. He leaned back against the booth and closed his eyes.

"We'll talk again," Tournier said, squeezing the older man's arm in a friendly fashion. Then he left, leaving five dollars on the table.

14

THE student body had obviously been filing out of the building for some time when Lambert arrived. The girls huddled in groups of twos, fives, eights, their parochial school wine-red jackets worn loosely, as if they were artist's smocks.

A man with a red face waited for him on the brick steps.

"I thought it would be best to dismiss them," he said, and then added that his name was Pryor.

"What's up?" asked Lambert.

But Pryor had turned and was walking away swiftly. Lambert followed him, down a corridor and up three narrow flights of stairs. Lambert had forgotten the narrowness and constriction of school stairs—the scene of perpetual fights and liaisons of all kinds—and he grew gloomy at the recollection as he climbed.

They walked down another corridor toward a group of adults—teachers—who were clustered in front of an enormous old-fashioned bathroom door, with slats, on which GIRLS was printed.

As the group spotted Pryor and Lambert coming toward them, they moved away from the door.

Their faces were ashen with fear.

Pryor raised one hand, and then brought the hand downward in a dramatic fashion—pointing.

He was pointing at a thin river of blood that was trickling beneath the bottom of the slat door and wandering into the corridor.

Pryor said: "About an hour ago a young girl named Joanne Swift went to the bathroom. She didn't return. Her teacher went to find out what had happened. Mrs. Lee. She didn't return. When another teacher went to investigate, she heard Mrs. Lee scream out that no one should come in . . . that no one under any circumstances should come in."

Lambert took out his weapon and held it down and away from his body.

"You can still hear Mrs. Lee. Can you hear Mrs. Lee?" Pryor asked.

He was right. A distinctive moan could be heard, long and low and almost whistling.

Lambert said to Pryor: "Have you called for an ambulance?"

"No."

"Well, do it now."

Pryor ran down the hallway to a phone. The teachers were staring at Lambert. He stared back at them.

"What's the name of the teacher in there, again?" He asked.

"Mrs. Lee."

"I mean her first name."

"Carol."

Lambert nodded. He moved closer to the door.

"Carol? Don't worry, I'm a police officer. I'm coming in, Carol, okay?"

He crouched and moved through the swinging door quickly.

A woman was lying on the floor not two feet from him, on the scrubbed white tile.

She didn't seem to be hurt or wounded; she appeared to be in shock, her arms folded, moaning and rocking and staring at the ceiling.

His gun high now, Lambert scrambled over to the woman. She didn't focus her eyes on him.

"Everything's okay," Lambert said to her. "You're going to be all right. Where's the girl?"

He noticed that there was a thick stripe of blood across the bathroom floor that was dribbling out into the hall. With his eyes he followed the trail in the other direction, up to the row of sinks.

He started to rise from his squatting position next to Carol Lee.

He stopped. The weapon suddenly became limp in his hand.

On the third sink from the left was perched a human head . . . the head of a young girl.

It had been severed completely from its body.

One eye seemed to have vanished, the socket

filled with a dark gore. The other eye rolled wildly . . . it refused to die with the body.

Lambert broke his gaze away, flushed and nauseated, unable to move.

"Is everything all right in there?" He heard Pryor's voice.

"Everything is going to be okay," he called back, but his voice was too tremulous and he had to repeat himself to make himself heard, and then he added: "Just stay outside for a moment."

Lambert crawled toward the cubicles. He opened the first one. There was no one inside, only some graffiti on the wall about a teacher named John who had a penis thirty inches long.

The second cubicle was empty.

He opened the third cubicle, and he cried out and stuffed his face into his sleeve, turning around away from it.

The torso of a young girl was perched on a toilet. The head and arms and legs were gone.

Crazed, he ran to the next one and flung it open, and then the next one and flung it open.

He started to shout now—because these cubicles were filled with the severed limbs, legs and arms and God knows what else flung haphazardly into the corners.

He sat down on the floor with an enormous sense of shame, because he knew he was losing control of himself; he fiddled desperately with his fingers to put the safety on his weapon, and then he remembered nothing—saw nothing.

When he became conscious again the first thing

he saw was a stretcher carrying Mrs. Lee out of the bathroom.

Two uniformed policemen were gathering body parts in plastic bags.

He felt comfortable, at ease, and then he realized that he was resting against one wall and several blankets had been placed there to form a sort of cushion.

He looked at the row of sinks. The head was gone; the only thing that remained was a large splotch of red gore where it had lain.

He saw Pryor peer in and wave sorrowfully at him. Lambert waved feebly back.

He inspected his own clothes and was greatly relieved he hadn't vomited; it was bad enough to have passed out.

"I just can't leave you alone," said Tournier with a grin as he knelt beside Lambert.

"Sorry, Chief."

"For what?" Tournier was staring at the bathroom, a quadrant at a time. "I got here late," he said. "Tell me what you saw."

"Mrs. Lee, the teacher, was in shock on the floor. Then I saw a head on the sink." He paused.

"Then what?" Tournier prodded him.

"I started looking through the cubicles. And I saw the torso. No arms. No legs."

Lambert started to cry. He couldn't help himself. Tournier said nothing, just squatted there beside him even though his legs were beginning to ache.

"And then?"

"In the last two cubicles, over there, were the legs and arms and I don't know what else."

Tournier stood up.

"I thought Matt Novick was in the Vegas area, Chief," said Lambert.

"So did I," Tournier replied.

He raised a hand to signal Lambert that he should stay where he was, and that he, Tournier, would be back in a minute. Then the chief walked to where the uniformed policemen were packing the evidence to be transported to the lab. They were trying to maintain a distance, their faces set in noncommittal masks.

Tournier could see one mangled severed arm lying in a plastic bag with a label on it.

He moved closer to it slowly, as if he were approaching a plague victim. The fingers on the hand were pale and washed out; they could have been the fingers of anyone, any age. But he knew they were the fingers of thirteen-year-old Joanne Swift. That he had been told.

His eyes started to travel up the arm to the shoulder, to where it had been severed. He saw something halfway up, a deep ragged contusion. He bent over. It was on the girl's forearm, about two inches down from the elbow joint. It looked like a bite; it looked like some kind of teeth had fastened on the forearm, even for an instant, and then ripped away.

He started to walk back. Was it the same maniac? If it was, the progression was continuing. Each murder had been a little less neat; each horror a little less perfectly executed. This child's

limbs had not been surgically severed—she had
been ripped apart in a torrent of blood and sinew
and gore. And teeth—were they teeth marks? No
such marks had appeared on the other victims.
What, if anything, was the connection?

A man he didn't know was talking to Lambert.
He introduced himself to Tournier as the prin-
cipal of Cathedral, Pryor.

"Can you tell me how all this started?" Tournier asked.

"I told the detective," Pryor said, pointing
sadly at Lambert, who had not yet risen.

"Tell it again," Tournier said, and added: "If
you don't mind."

"The girl asked to go to the bathroom and was
given a pass."

God, Tournier thought, sixty years ago when
he was in school they had used passes to go to
the bathroom. It astonished him that nothing had
changed.

"She didn't come back. So the teacher, Mrs.
Lee, went to find her. She must have collapsed
inside and gone into shock when she saw what
had happened."

"Could I get you some water?" Pryor asked
Lambert. Detective Lambert shook his head and
heaved himself to his feet.

"I'm okay," he declared.

The three of them walked slowly out of the
bathroom and into Pryor's office. Tournier saw
the coffee machine and poured himself a cup. He
noted that Pryor was extremely composed for an

administrator, one of whose students had just
been ripped apart and flung about a bathroom.

But when Pryor was seated next to him, also
drinking some coffee, Tournier realized the man
was extremely confused, and it was the confusion
that gave him the semblance of calm.

Lambert, on the other hand, had not yet recovered, and it would be a long time before he
really did. He was sitting, quietly, but his eyes
were constantly moving—they kept darting
about the room—to Tournier, to Pryor, to the
wall, to the coffee machine. From time to time
he would reach down and pull at his trousers
near the knee, straightening the crease.

Pryor said: "I don't know how we are going to
clean the bathroom. I mean, the janitors don't
come until the evening, and by that time all the
blood and everything will be caked . . . dried
into the tile."

It was the type of stupid statement that someone invariably makes in the midst of a tragedy.
Tournier had heard variations of them all his life
as a cop; after fatal bank robberies; after finding
murder victims; after horrendous traffic acci-
dents. Someone always said something so stupid,
so outside the comprehension of everyone else
given the circumstances, that it was taken as an
utterly normal statement.

"Oh, my God," Pryor suddenly shouted, "no
one called her mother."

Tournier placed the empty coffee cup on the
desk, leaned back in the chair, and closed his
eyes. He wanted to stretch both arms out and

embrace Lambert, but he did nothing. The two police officers watched as the administrator began to fiddle with his small office computer—carefully typing in the name of the victim and then writing down the telephone number of the child as it appeared on the screen.

"I'm going to call now," he said hesitantly, looking at Tournier for some kind of help. Tournier could give him none.

15

EDMONTON was a tough team. What they lacked in power they made up in speed and pitching. In addition, they had lost five out of their first six games and they came ready to play Oaktown, mean.

The first two innings were scoreless, and the stadium settled in for what was obviously going to be a pitcher's duel. There was a good crowd on hand but not a full house.

"The team wants to do something about Larrabee," Bunny said.

Dominic nodded, encouraging her to go on. He didn't much feel like talking, but he could listen; he could always do that. And he didn't know what she was talking about. The entire team had attended the funeral. What else could they do for Larrabee—he was dead.

"I was thinking about one of those patches with the man's initials, sewn on the arm or wrist, like the L. A. Dodgers did when their pitching coach died."

"Why not?" Dominic shrugged. But he really found the notion bizarre. Larrabee had been crushed to death by some kind of horror, his stomach slit open, the viscera removed. It was more than a normal death, a normal loss. It just wasn't appropriate to put his initials on one's arm. It was just something one feels—this inappropriateness.

"And maybe a scholarship fund," said Bunny. She was obviously getting all worked up about this; she was beginning to talk quickly, almost compulsively; outlining all kinds of possibilities.

In the fifth inning the game began to open up. Dwyer, the Wolves' left fielder, got their first hit of the game; a clean double down the right-field line. Loors walked. Then Sisco, the Wolves' shortstop, laid down a beautiful bunt between the pitcher and first base and there was no play at all. The bases were loaded. Battaglia struck out. Ardmore flied out to center, allowing one run and the other runners to advance on the throw home. With two out and two on, the Wolves' catcher, Timken, stepped up.

"He was such a crazy, funny man," said Bunny, speaking about Larrabee, and then she choked up, unable to say any more.

"That he was," Dominic said. There were always flakes on teams, Dominic thought, and over the years he had seen much worse than Larrabee. The trouble with flakes was that no matter how funny they were, how much they helped cut tension on and off the field, how their bizarre exploits made good newspaper headlines and kept the game in perspective—sooner or later there was big trouble; a nasty fight, an injury, racial remarks, something that always turned the joke sour and mean.

The Edmonton manager decided to bring in a relief pitcher after a delayed conference on the mound, which sent the Oaktown fans into a jeering, hooting frenzy. Timken stepped out of the batter's box and began to apply the pine tar to his bat, methodically and thoughtfully.

Dominic found himself looking intently about the stadium. He realized he was searching for Jackie Cannon. It was absurd. He had no idea if that drunk went to games; and even if he wanted to, how could he afford the admission?

Dominic was watching the game in front of him with great detachment, almost as if he were a traveler in a foreign land. It was Jackie Cannon's words that had created this situation: Dominic could not get rid of the drunk's words— that they had won only death in 1963, and that even the championship had been bought. The words festered in him. They clattered away in his head like empty bottles. Above all, they made the game itself seem like a threat that he was watching unfold; he watched with detachment, with calmness, but each pitch was possibly lethal—not to the batter but to the world. It seemed that a lifetime of joy and participation was shriveling into a nasty little ball of terror, all of it unfathomable.

The Edmonton relief pitcher finished his warm-up pitches. Timken stepped back into the batter's box. The pitch was high and outside. Timken stepped across the plate and poked it between first and second. Two more runs scored. The stadium went wild.

In the seventh, Oaktown went ahead 6–1 and Roger brought in Tim Shea to finish up.

"I have my doubts about this guy holding any lead," Bunny said to Dominic, nastily.

He stared at her, startled. Bunny usually did not speak like that. And then he realized, sheepishly, that she was trying to deflect her affection away. It dawned on him that Bunny would only say that if she was sleeping with Shea; to keep people off the track. In other times he would have good-naturedly pursued it with fervor, bantering with her that Shea really should be run out of baseball and sent to a road gang, until her affection broke through and she defended him. But he hadn't the slightest inclination to be playful now; in fact, her words were like tin. The bloody game was like tin.

He got up suddenly, said the game was a lock, and he would meet them, as usual, at Victor's.

"Are you sick?" Bunny asked, concerned.

"Just need a drink," he said, "need to warm up."

"Rog and I will meet you there after the game."

He nodded and threaded his way through the aisles to the exit.

When he reached Victor's he sat in his usual

booth and ordered just a beer, sipping it in the
half darkness.

The bar was empty except for a man and a
woman in a booth toward the front. They were
seated side by side and the woman had her hand
on the man's shoulder, reaching up to play with
his hair from time to time.

He wondered if Shea and Bunny sat like that
in out-of-the-way bars. He wondered how Larrabee had been with women—poor Larrabee,
gutted. No human, no animal, no living thing
should ever be so defiled, he thought. He shiv-
ered. He remembered the ball girl, Alice
Draught—the way she did her acrobatic cartwheel after catching a ball. She probably had
become the ball girl only to be applauded for her
gymnastic ability. She probably couldn't have
cared less about how many balls she caught.
Who, in Jackie Cannon's words, had won death
for her? Who was to blame?

He stared past the couple, out through the
window onto the street. Who was out there now?
Who would be next? What horror was waiting
. . . what mutilation . . . what awesome power
that could rip living beings apart as if they were
pieces of twine?

His neck was tight; he reached back to massage
it and then pulled his hand frontward quickly,
as if he had touched fire. The mere touch of his
neck had reminded him of the red mark on the
victims; and the red mark that Walter Bunsen
had laughingly requested to be applied to the

ballplayers' necks in 1963—the year that Oak-town won it all.

His memory was now so bad that Dominic wondered if he, as the manager, had also put some red on his neck, some pig's blood, or cow's blood, or was it just paint?

But the marks on Larrabee and Alice Draught had been their own blood applied by the tongue of the beast . . . or someone or something that could think rationally in the midst of all that dismemberment. He wished Tournier was in the bar with him now; the chief was cryptic, but Dominic trusted him.

He looked out the window again. There were more people. The game must be over. He caught glimpses of their shoulders and faces in the dim streetlights. People started coming into the bar. And then he saw Bunny and Rog walking toward the booth.

They sat down across from him. They were agitated, excited, ill at ease.

"Did you hear about the girl?" Bunny asked.

"No."

Roger said: "We heard it on the radio. A girl was murdered at the parochial school, in the bathroom."

Dominic saw Bunny staring at him. He realized that Roger didn't know all the facts about the other murders; he didn't know about the mutilations, although he may have heard the rumors.

But this time the radio had gone further.

"They said the child's body was mutilated,"

Bunny said, "so badly that one of the teachers who went into the bathroom to find her is in shock in Oaktown General."

The bartender, who always worked nights of a game, brought over three bottles of beer.

"Did we win?" Dominic asked.

"Who cares?" Roger exploded. "What the hell is the matter with you, Dominic?"

Dominic ignored him and sipped some beer. Bunny said: "They gave her name on the radio, but I don't remember it. God, it just slipped away. What was her name, Roger?"

"Swift. Her last name was Swift."

"Joanne, that's right, Joanne Swift."

"Who won the game?" Dominic persisted.

"Goddammit, we won, Dominic," Roger shouted.

Dominic raised one hand to caution Roger to lower his voice.

"How did Shea pitch?"

Roger and Bunny stared at each other as if Dominic were crazy. They stopped talking. Dominic closed his eyes. They sat in silence. Around them the noise level of the bar rose. All the booths had quickly been filled. The long bar was three-deep. The jukebox had been turned on and was playing a country and western song by Willie Nelson.

"What was her name?" Dominic asked.

"Joanne Swift."

"Joanne Swift," Dominic said, and then he repeated it two or three more times.

"How old was she?" he asked.

"Thirteen or fourteen, I think the radio said," Bunny answered.

"At Cathedral?" Dominic asked.

"Yeah, the parochial school. You know it," Roger replied testily.

"And they said she was mutilated?" Dominic asked.

"That's what they said," Roger affirmed.

Bunny reached out across the table and grasped Dominic's hand. The hands held tightly. Then Dominic disengaged.

He had to get out of there. He had to find Jackie Cannon. He had to speak to him; to ask him to explain; to ask for help.

Dominic closed his eyes. He tried to imagine a face on the little girl murdered in the bathroom. How had the mutilation happened this time? What fresh horrors littered the walls?

"Where are you going, Coach?" Roger asked as the older man stood up.

Dominic patted him on the shoulder and smiled at Bunny.

"Just need some air, folks, I'm fine," he said, and walked out a bit unsteadily—the noise and the crowd making his head pound and the smoke suddenly smarting his eyes until they teared.

He started to walk away from the bar and in the opposite direction from the stadium. He started to walk toward that bar in the Armory District where he had bumped into Jackie Cannon by chance.

He walked quickly, feeling the urgency in his legs. When he reached the statue of Travis Wyatt—the Oaktown boy who had received the Congressional Medal of Honor, posthumously, for his service in World War II—he realized he had made the wrong turn somewhere. He was way east of the Armory District, near the railroad terminal and tracks that had been abandoned years ago. The mist was starting to move in.

He crossed the main road and stood at the edge of the shrub field, littered with garbage. He could see the long line of decaying freight cars that had been lined up there for almost as long as he had been in Oaktown.

The freight cars were sad-looking, like lost dreams, each one stenciled with the name of a defunct railroad line. Some were red, some rust, some brown, some decayed yellow—and some were old refrigerator cars with that distinctive ribbing.

The sight of those cars seemed to mesmerize him with memories of childhood; of standing by his window late at night and waiting for the night train; waiting for that long, low whistle and then the chug, chug, chug as it crawled up the hill, steel glistening in the moonlight, smoke curling high.

He crossed the field and stood in front of a car.

Suddenly, on the side of the car, he saw a shadow projected from the shrub trees behind him and the streetlights behind them.

It loomed large against the crumbling freight car, black, inchoate.

Then, as he stared at it, it took form!

He could make out a man in a distinctive pose. He stared at it for the longest while until he realized the shadow was his, a silhouette of himself at bat when he was young. Yes, he could make out that distinctive batting stance—the front leg splayed wide in the way that everyone used to laugh at.

I'm going crazy, he laughed to himself, I'm seeing myself everywhere.

Suddenly, every freight car displayed the same shadow—of himself.

He shut his eyes tightly and opened them again; the shadows were gone.

He felt ashamed of all this foolishness. He had to get back to the Armory District and that bar . . . he had to find Jackie Cannon.

Dominic started to move back across the field, which was scattered with an inconceivable assembly of junk.

A sound came suddenly from behind his right shoulder.

Rats, he thought, this place must be overrun with rats.

The sound exploded into a high-pitched cry that froze him to the spot.

The cry became a scream, and then a sound so horrible, so filled with loathing and blood and a world he had never seen, that he fell to his knees—forehead wreathed with sweat, every part of his body trembling.

The sound vanished. He started to rise. It came again. He froze.

He knew that it was for him; that now he

would have to pay; that now his body would be ripped to shreds; that he, too, would now suffer the indescribable pain of mutilation by a beast that had no name.

He heard it behind him, enormous, filled with the night and the past and its hate.

It was there. He could feel it. He could not turn. He could not face it.

And then he heard it move in the darkness. But it was neither moving toward him nor away from him.

It was moving in rhythmic fashion. The wind began to swirl. The trees bent.

He understood. It was dancing. It was dancing before it struck.

Now, he thought. Now he must move. He started to run—toward the light, toward the main road.

It was very close to him now. His nostrils were filled with fear. His legs were heavy. He could see the road. He cried out, his chest bursting.

He reached the light. A car screeched its brakes and swerved out of the way, its fender hitting Dominic and sending him head over heels into the center of the road.

He saw the driver's face before he passed out— the face reminded him of his father.

16

TOURNIER sat on a straight-backed chair in front of the bed in Room 310 of Oaktown General and waited for the old man to awake.

He remembered that he had told Dominic in the coffee shop that he would recall for him the stories his grandmother used to tell him about the man called Garnier.

Tournier leaned forward in his chair and placed his chin in both hands. No, he wouldn't tell Dominic, there was no point, but he could remember himself; he would always remember because his grandmother had read to him from a big red book that had always fascinated him. She kept this book locked away as if it were a Bible. It wasn't a Bible—he never knew what it was or where it finally rested. His mother told him after his grandmother died that the big red book had been burned as it should have been.

She had read to him in her theatrical voice: "Garnier, tried and condemned by the parlia-

ment of Dole, being in the shape of a werewolf,
caught a girl of ten or twelve years in a vineyard
of Chastenoy, a quarter of a league from Dole,
and having slain her with his teeth and clawlike
hands, he ate part of her flesh and carried the
rest to his wife. A month later, in the same form,
he took another girl, and would have eaten her
also, had he not, as he himself confessed, been
prevented by three persons who happened to be
passing by; and a fortnight after he strangled a
boy of ten in the vineyard of Gredisan, and ate
his flesh; and in the form of a man and not of a
wolf, he killed another boy of twelve or thirteen
years in a wood of the village of Porouse with the
intention of eating him but was again prevented.
He was condemned to be burned, and the sentence was executed."

Tournier grinned at how very well he had remembered most of the ancient tale. But his
grandmother had recited this yarn to him hundreds of times, and other similar yarns too. But
it was after she caught him masturbating that she
read it to him with great emphasis and warned
him against the dangers of "self-abuse," which
she said would lead to melancholia and which
would then lead to the horrors of lycanthropy,
which he never understood until years later.

I am thinking like a kook, Tournier thought,
and he knew he had been since he saw that first
body. But now he was not alone—the rumors had
begun to snowball: extraterrestrials, vampires,
werewolves, and the whole bizarre lunatic imagination of Western America in its most perverse

vein. And here he was—Police Chief Tournier—
supposedly the voice of reason . . . of propriety
. . . of law and order . . . here he was, obsessed
with an old grandmother's lunacy.

The old man turned and groaned. All Tournier
knew was that the old man had been found on
the roadside across from the abandoned railroad
terminal. It seemed he had run suddenly out onto
the road and been walloped by an oncoming vehicle. Amazingly, Dominic had suffered no broken bones whatsoever; nothing but a pattern of
deep bruises up and down one side of his body.

Dominic's eyes opened. Tournier pulled the
chair closer and sat down on it. He wondered
what the hell Dominic had been doing in that
part of the city.

"How do you feel?" Tournier asked.

"Tired."

"They gave you something for the pain, but
those bruises will take a long time to heal."

Dominic beckoned for Tournier to come closer,
and the old man's eyes darted toward the door
and the bathroom to make sure no one else was
there.

"I heard it. I sensed it. It was behind me,
there, in the lot, by the road. It was coming for
me, Tournier."

The fear in the old man's voice was powerful,
persuasive.

"Who, Dominic? Who came for you?"

"Listen, Tournier. It was dancing."

"Dancing?"

"I could hear it dancing, behind me, and then I ran."

Tournier squirmed in his seat. Since this mess had started he had not known up from down; he had vacillated between the belief that Matt Novick was a prime suspect and that some horrible conspiracy existed that was beyond his experience and his knowledge.

But now it was becoming absurd. Now the killer or killers were dancing.

"What were you doing down there?" Tournier asked.

"I was looking for Jackie Cannon."

"In the railroad yards?"

"No, I got lost. I left Victor's after Roger and Bunny told me what had happened to that girl at the school, and I started walking to the Armory District, but I got lost."

"The girl's name was Joanne Swift."

"I know that," Dominic said, "but the mark—was it there again? The red mark on the base of the neck?"

"On this one, Dominic, we can't tell. The body was literally ripped apart."

"Ripped apart?"

"Yes. Head on the sink. A leg here. An arm there."

Sudden silence descended on the white hospital room. Tournier was astonished that he was now able to speak very calmly and very clinically about the most horrendous sights he had ever seen. If a rational human could speak like that, he reasoned, a rational human could mutilate like that.

"I was supposed to be next. I knew it as I stood there."

"Why you, Dominic?"

"Nineteen sixty-three."

He was starting to ramble again, Tournier thought, all about what that drunken half-breed ballplayer told him. Something about winning only death.

"But you saw nothing coming toward you, Dominic, you saw nothing."

"No, I saw nothing."

"Why didn't you turn? Why didn't you get a glimpse of it?"

"You don't believe me, do you, Tournier? If you believed I was telling the truth, you would not ask that question. Because I was afraid. Because it seems to be coming from all around you, as if it has risen from the earth and the sky at the same time. I was afraid because it was like a wind, a smell, a river of scent that you cannot really see or hear or touch."

"Calm down, Dominic, relax. I'm not saying I don't believe you."

"The only thing you would have believed were the chunks of my body that you found—here and there, and hanging on a tree limb."

"Yes," Tournier said, sadly, "I would have believed that."

"Time, Tournier, there was no time. I thought only of seconds . . . of the seconds I had to live. I cannot make you understand."

Dominic lay back in his bed exhausted, his eyes closed. One of his buttocks had begun to throb, like someone was pounding it with a very heavy mallet. He turned on one side.

"There is something else, Tournier. Before I sensed him, before I knew that I was next, there were shadows on the freight cars."

"Shadows?"

"Yes, like shadows on a wall. But they were shadows of myself fifty years ago or more."

"Of Dominic Lombardi?"

"Right. Of me. They were shadows of me at the plate; it was my stance, my uniform."

"What uniform?"

"The old San Francisco Seals."

"DiMaggio's team," mused Tournier. He didn't know what to make of the shadows at all. He couldn't respond to Dominic's recounting.

"I think the shadows were to lure me down there, by the freight cars. And there it would happen."

Again there was silence. Tournier stared about the room. He remembered that the teacher who had discovered Joanne Swift's dismembered body was in the same hospital, on the same floor, sedated.

"Tell me more about the girl," Dominic finally said, with a groan, as if he had given up trying to explain what had happened.

"Lambert got the call when we were in the coffee shop together. He found what was left of her."

"Not Matt Novick this time, huh? Matt Novick

is heading northeast with two companions after rampages in Reno and Vegas."

"He could double back," Tournier noted.

"And I could hit safely in fifty-seven straight games," said Dominic scornfully.

"Her grandfather, the girl's grandfather, used to be head of the Department of Public Works in Oaktown. In the late fifties, early sixties, I think. Louis Swift. He was indicted on charges of corruption in the late sixties and died waiting out an appeal."

"Louis Swift." Dominic was rolling the sound on his tongue.

"You knew him?"

"Heard of him."

"Well, this is the first one with no connection to the Oaktown Wolves. So I was right. The other connections are just coincidence."

Tournier reached out to the bedside table for some water. His chair scraped the floor. When he turned back Dominic had his hands clasped over his ears and his face was as white as death.

"That sound," Dominic whispered, "it was something like that."

"Like what?"

"Like the chair scraping on the floor. Oh, it was like that, only a thousand times louder and deeper and it sounded like it came from someone's stomach. And it seemed to come faster behind me . . . real fast . . . and the air around was beginning to glow. Do you know what I mean, Tournier, glow?"

Tournier drank some of the tepid water and

made sure his chair did not make that noise again.

"I have to go, Dominic," he said, after he had finished the water.

"Not yet," Dominic said.

"Okay."

"I have something else to tell you."

"Okay," Tournier repeated, his visit now fatiguing him greatly.

"Louis Swift, Joanne Swift's grandfather, was a drinking buddy of Walter Bunsen's."

"Who?"

"Walter Bunsen. Hell, he was the team's owner in 1963, Tournier, don't you remember anything?"

Tournier nodded. He looked directly at Dominic, as if to question whether it was possible the older man was making this up.

"Are you sure?"

"I'm sure."

"But did he have anything to do with the team other than have a few drinks with the owner? I mean, Alice Draught was a ball girl and her grandfather was the team trainer. Poor Larrabee played on the team. I mean, there has to be a stronger connection than that."

"It's strong enough to see Jackie Cannon, isn't it?"

Tournier nodded. The old man was making sense, good sense. He realized he was being stubborn. No matter what or who the beast was who was mutilating and murdering and dismembering, his job was to investigate links—each and every one.

"Where can we find him?"

"I don't know the name. But I know the place."

"Lambert will pick me up. I can go myself. We don't need you. Rest. Give me a full description, and then rest."

"I give you nothing. I go or you don't find him. I want out of here. Out."

Dominic swung his legs over the side of the bed, his face twisted into a grimace of pain. He took a step, and then another step, and soon he was walking gingerly around the room, testing the bruised limbs.

"Once you get them moving, they'll be fine," Tournier said. "It's tomorrow morning that the trouble will start."

Dominic found his clothes in the closet and dressed slowly. When he was finished, he sat down, out of breath, on the edge of the bed. Tournier had called Lambert and the detective would be there shortly.

Tournier took out a small cigar and chewed it reflectively without lighting it. An alcoholic old ballplayer tells a frightened old man that the horrors around them all come from a single stupid baseball season a quarter of a century ago. Has there ever been a longer long shot? Particularly for Tournier, who didn't give a damn about baseball or any other sport except maybe for dogsled racing, which he liked to watch on television.

He lit the cigar and stole a glance at Dominic, who was seated, fully dressed, on the edge of the bed. Tournier could see that the old man was still terror-stricken; he had that funny vacant stare that victims have—the ungazing blink, the desperation to take one's eyes out of the feeling process because they had betrayed oneself.

Tournier realized that he must now purge from his mind everything that stank of the paranormal: his grandmother's wisdom; his colleagues' speculations; the bizarre evidence. Only reason—a cop's reason—would enable him to reach the truth. He forced himself to look at Dominic again, this time almost clinically.

Something, obviously, had spooked the old man. Something had probably been behind him on that lot, in front of those corpses of freight cars. But it was not what or who had destroyed Joanne Swift. Joanne Swift had not lived long enough to be terrified. What there remained of her consciousness in this world was in the bloodstains that were splattered the length and width of the old bathroom. The sadness of that was almost as unbearable as the horror.

17

USUALLY Bunny wanted to make love in the morning. And now it was morning. And Tim Shea was lying beside her. And she knew he was awake; all she had to do was touch him, anywhere, and he would move close to her. She didn't feel like making love this morning, although there had been plenty of lovemaking during the night. It was always that way when Tim had a good outing on relief—winning turned him on.

But she just lay there and did not extend a hand. She was worried about Dominic. He had acted very peculiarly in the bar, standing up suddenly and just walking out. She didn't remember him doing something like that ever before.

She understood that the girl's death had unnerved him; it had unnerved them all.

A powerful cramp suddenly gripped her right foot and she stiffened for a moment from the pain. Then the cramp vanished as quickly as it had come. Cramps and muscle pains had become common for her lately. She attributed it to anxiety from the murders. She wondered, as she lay there, where she had put the aspirin.

Shea turned over suddenly, moved toward her, and thrust his hand between her thighs, gently. She didn't move. She didn't respond.

"Why are you staring at me like that?" he asked.

"I didn't know I was staring."

"You are."

She opened her legs a bit to allow his hand to become more friendly.

"Sometimes, lately," he continued, "I see you staring at me, and I have the strangest feeling that you're looking at Larrabee."

"That's not funny," she said, "and besides, I wasn't thinking about Larrabee. I was thinking about that girl."

"The one in the school?"

She nodded and closed her eyes. He moved closer, and she felt him kiss her breast.

"If I think about Larrabee," said Tim Shea, "I am unable to move. If I think about him, I can't even cry. I just feel like someone hit me over the head with a bat."

He was getting into a remorseful erotic mood, which she liked, alternating between depression and elation.

"What really happened to Larrabee?" he asked suddenly.

"He was murdered."

"But what happened to him?"

She had never told him that she had identified the body. She had never told him what Dominic had described: the stomach slit open and emptied. Empty Larrabee, murdered and befouled.

She felt strange. She accepted his hand and his mouth. She wanted him to make love to her again, but she was strangely distracted. She was beginning to feel a sense of doom around her, around them, around the team, around the city—perhaps around the world. It seemed to be creeping in over the Coast Range and mutilating all of them.

"Who would do that to a child?" she asked, opening her eyes.

"I don't know," Tim answered, moving away from her a bit, but keeping his hand between her legs, touching her. He didn't know what she wanted now.

"It's funny," she said, "I dreamed about my father last night. I just remembered it now. He looked in the dream like that picture I saw of him at the political convention before I was born. He was standing with a candidate and grinning like a Cheshire cat, and he was wearing one of those stupid old-fashioned straw hats.

"I've seen pictures of your father. There's one in the clubhouse office."

Bunny suddenly flung herself onto Tim's chest, grasping him fiercely. She wanted to be held, tightly. He held her. They lay like that for a long while, not saying a word.

It was not recalling the dream about her father that had frightened her. It was the strange feelings about her father that had begun to surface in her consciousness. She felt that he was somehow in contact with her, from the grave. She felt in some odd way that he inhabited his grave without decaying . . . that he was in the ground but not a corpse. It was unfathomable.

Then she whispered into his ear: "What happens if one of us is next? What happens if it's you or me? Don't you feel like we're next?"

"Hell, no," he replied.

"Why not us?"

"Why not anyone?"

"I don't love you, Tim, but right now I need you."

Tim laughed, nervously, and his hand reached around to caress her buttocks.

"That's why I like you, Bunny, you always say the wrong thing to me."

"At least I can find the plate," she quipped.

Tim let out an enormous war whoop and rolled her over so that she was precariously perched on the edge of the bed. As she hung there, frightened and childlike at first, she felt a growing sense of absurdity—the absurdity of their erotic games, which meant nothing . . . while all around them was blood and the promise of more blood.

Why, she thought, was everything becoming unreal except the game of baseball? Was that what my father was all about?

18

"**T**HIS is it," said Dominic as the three men stood just inside the bar. "I remember the bartender and the walls. This is it."

They walked over to the bar, behind which the bartender was removing bottles of beer from cartons, stuffing the bottles into large tubs of ice beneath the counter, and then folding the empty cartons and flinging them over the bar for someone to sweep out. There were few people drinking. It was a bit too early for that bar, which did not begin its real activity until early evening.

Lambert flashed his badge and the bartender straightened up. Dominic told him who he was looking for; he reminded the bartender of the trouble he'd had with Jackie Cannon the night he was there. It jogged his memory.

"Sure, I know that guy. He staggers in here about three or four times a week. Sometimes he has money, sometimes he tries to hustle a drink off the paying customers and I have to boot him out. He's not a bad guy. He's an alkie."

"Was he here yesterday, or today?"

"No."

"When?"

"I remember you now," the bartender said to Dominic, "and, in fact, I haven't seen that character since you were here with him."

They got back into the car and made a tour of all bars in the Armory and surrounding districts. They walked through short stretches of abandoned streets where Oaktown derelicts traditionally hung out. They went to the bus station and the small airport and other locations where Oaktown drunks tended to panhandle. No luck.

Finally, they pulled off the road and sat exhausted in the car in the early evening, behind the smokestacks of the local utility building.

Lambert asked: "Where next?"

Tournier half turned around to Dominic, who was seated alone in the back of the large unmarked police car; one of the three unmarked cars owned and maintained by the Oaktown police department. He studied Dominic for a moment, who seemed to have grown more and more abstract and withdrawn as the hours passed. The pain in his legs, thought Tournier, or a reaction to the painkillers.

"Dominic," Tournier finally said, nudging the old man out of his reverie—"where next?"

"I don't know."

"Maybe those warehouse lots where the super-

markets load their trucks," said Lambert, trying
to be helpful.

There was no reply from Dominic, so Tournier
signaled Lambert to go there. The car drove off
again.

"When's the little girl's funeral? When's Joanne
Swift's funeral?"

"Probably tomorrow," Tournier said.

Dominic laughed a harsh, ugly laugh. "Who's
going to put her together? Huh? Or are they just
going to drop her piece by piece into the coffin?"

"I imagine the coffin will be closed," Tournier
said.

"Will they bury her in her uniform?"

"What uniform?"

Dominic, for some reason, had been thinking
of a baseball uniform, but then realized the
thought was absurd, and said: "The uniform the
kids who go to parochial school wear."

"Who knows?" Tournier responded.

They were cruising the warehouse areas now.
The wide blank walls of the warehouses made
Dominic think of the freight cars. He shrank back
a bit in his seat, half expecting to see those shadows again; half expecting to hear that sound of
a living, breathing horror behind him . . . hungry for him . . . ready to rip him to pieces. His
forehead was suddenly covered with sweat.

"What's the matter, Dominic?"

Dominic didn't answer.

"Stop the car," Tournier ordered, and Lambert pulled the vehicle over.

Tournier turned in the front seat so that he

was facing Dominic. "You shouldn't have left
the hospital so soon. I shouldn't have let you do
it."

"No, it's not that," Dominic replied, "it's the
other thing."

"What other thing?"

"In the railroad yard . . . what was coming for
me."

Tournier turned to face front again and motioned to Lambert to start the car.

"Where to?" Lambert asked.

"I don't know. Any ideas, Dominic?"

"No."

"Just cruise," Tournier said, and he sank back
in the seat and closed his eyes.

They drove in larger and larger circles, cross-
ing the main arteries from north to south. No one
spoke. All of them knew that they had nothing
concrete except the next death . . . wherever and
whenever that would come . . . except for the
next mutilation, wherever and whenever that
would come.

Then Tournier turned to Lambert, exasper-
ated. "Where the hell would you go if you were
a sick, crazy alkie . . . you had no money, no
shelter, no booze . . . where would you crawl
to?"

"I'd check into a drying-out tank," said Lambert, and the moment he spoke those words, everyone in the car knew he was right . . . it was
possible . . . it was the first and last place they
should have looked.

"St. Elizabeth's," said Tournier, "just this side of the county line."

It was a twenty-minute ride to the small, bright hospital called St. Elizabeth's. It had maintained a walk-in detox program for more than thirty years; lately it had expanded to include treatment for addiction to other drugs, particularly cocaine and the amphetamines as well as alcohol. It was funded by a patchwork of federal, state, local, and private money; it was staffed by nuns, lay nurses, and physicians, and a wide variety of volunteers. No one had a bad word for St. Elizabeth's.

Lambert said: "I was here about two years ago on the Murdock case, Chief; the alcohol detox unit is that low building set way back."

"The blue one?"

"Right."

They pulled into the small parking lot, which abutted a low blue building that looked like a skating rink in shape.

A nurse greeted them at the front desk, quickly, as if they could be a threat, and then her practiced eyes roved along them trying to pick out which one was the potential patient, which one for detox.

Tournier showed her his shield, quickly, and they were all ushered to an alcove to await the appearance of Dr. Roth.

Roth came out five minutes later, a small cheerful man with an utterly bald or shaved head and eyeglasses that stayed up on his forehead. He wanted to know how he could be of help.

Lambert acted as spokesman: "We're trying
to locate an alcoholic named Jackie Cannon
who, if he is here, would have been admitted,
or admitted himself, within the past three
days."

Roth had a habit of continually taking a pencil
in and out of the pocket of his green tunic. Now
he pulled the pencil all the way out, raised it up,
and signaled that they should follow him.

They walked through swinging doors into the
ward. There were about twenty men lying in
beds in various stages of detox misery. Another
ten patients were wandering around. Everyone
wore bright bathrobes. Nurses were omnipresent
with carts and trays loaded with what seemed
like vitamin supplements.

Tournier and Lambert fell in step behind
Dominic as the older man walked slowly down
the aisle, studying the face of each patient. He
did not see Jackie Cannon.

Roth shrugged and led them through another
set of swinging doors into a ward that was totally empty of patients; beyond that was a row
of what seemed to be locked rooms with small
peepholes on the doors. Dominic peered into
each one.

After peering into the third room on his left,
he turned around and said: "That is, I think,
Jackie Cannon."

Roth opened the door and all four of them
walked inside. Jackie Cannon was in one corner,
on the floor, wrapped in a bizarre kind of sheet,
his hands and feet totally immobile.

"Full sheet restraint, I'm afraid," said Roth.

"What happened?" Tournier asked.

"He's been thrashing about . . . just a precaution to keep him from hurting himself and others," Roth answered.

"Why don't you just club him over the head?" inquired Lambert, sardonically.

Roth looked at him wearily and replied, "You are looking at a bad Stage Four withdrawal, which you probably know nothing about—so I'll excuse your totally ignorant remark."

There was silence. Then Roth recited in a singsong manner from some textbook in his past.

"Stage Four withdrawal. Delirium tremens. Onset is two to three days after cessation of drinking, up to ten days if other drugs are involved. Profound confusion and disorientation plus Stage Two withdrawal symptoms. Vivid hallucinations. DT's preceded by restlessness, irritability, tremulousness with deterioration in mental status. Increased blood pressure, increased pulse, increased temperature. DT's is a medical emergency."

Tournier knelt beside the restrained man. The face was like that of a stroke victim—half calm, half contorted. The eyes were sleepy but moving; once in a while the body would be shaken by trembling. Spittle dribbled down one side of his mouth although Cannon went to great effort with his tongue to catch it.

"He's sedated," Roth said.

Tournier could smell Cannon's decay; it was

like smelling a very old and damp house; it was, above all, sour.

"I have to talk to him," Tournier said to Roth.

The doctor shrugged and said in a clipped official voice: "You must be kidding. Come back in two or three days. Leave him alone now. He's ill. Did you hear what I told you? Stage Four withdrawal is a medical emergency."

Tournier motioned with his hand for the doctor to crouch beside him. Roth looked confused. Tournier motioned again and the physician squatted next to the police chief, both of them very close to Jackie Cannon.

"Do you remember that girl murdered in the stadium?"

Roth nodded.

"Do you remember her name?" Tournier continued.

"No," said Roth.

"Her name was Alice Draught. During the murder she was mutilated while still alive."

"Are you telling me this poor fool had something to do with that?"

Roth stood up and looked at each of the three men in turn.

"Yes," said Tournier, "I am telling you exactly that."

Roth stared at him for a long time, as if trying to ascertain whether the man was telling the truth.

"I'll be close by," he finally said, and walked out.

Jackie Cannon was trying to roll now, his face

alternately flushing and growing pale. The sheets kept him from rolling, and all he could do was scrunch himself up against the wall. He stared at them, but no one could really tell if he saw them. He was making sounds, but they were not words.

"Dominic," Tournier said, and the old man came close and placed a hand, tenderly, on Jackie Cannon's shoulder. Then Dominic took out a handkerchief and wiped Jackie's face. Holding on to Tournier for support, Dominic then squatted down.

He started to speak to the alcoholic. "Tell me about 1963, Jackie. Tell me what happened. Tell me what you meant when you said we had won death."

There was no answer from Cannon, only an intense stare aimed at Dominic. Then he started to thrash violently. Tournier reached out and grasped the man's shoulder, to keep him steady, to help him. Cannon's face was beginning to contort again.

Dominic continued: "Another girl has been murdered, Jackie. A young girl. And there was a ballplayer, Larrabee. This is the third. Who is killing them, Jackie? Who is mutilating them? What is going on? Who is behind it? Jackie, listen to me. Someone tried to kill me yesterday. Me, Jackie. I was there in 1963. I managed. Have I won death also? What the hell is going on, Jackie?"

Jackie Cannon stopped struggling. The color

drained from his face. His tongue began to work furiously in his mouth.

"What's going on, Jackie? Help us. Tell us what you meant. Tell us what to do. We're begging you, Jackie. Don't let any more die."

Tournier stared at the ill man as Dominic's voice began to rise in passion and fury. Tournier suddenly felt a sense of power in Cannon; he had the sense that the ill man in front of him knew something very important . . . that he had locked in his brain a single key, a single phrase that would end all the horror. He now understood why Dominic had been so desperate to find him. He understood why Dominic had been so desperate to discover what the drunk meant when he said the 1963 team had "won death."

Cannon started to babble.

Lambert moved in close with the hand-held cassette recorder. He pressed it almost against the drunk's lips.

The three men listened but could not comprehend. Cannon's voice was cracking and the words tumbled out one after another in a slurred consistency.

Then he started to choke and Tournier rammed his fingers down Jackie Cannon's throat and pulled out a massive ball of thick saliva.

Cannon suddenly relaxed. But he talked no more.

The three men stepped back. Tournier turned and saw a face in the small window of the door. It was the physician, Roth. He nodded. Roth walked inside and checked Cannon.

"He's fine. He'll be okay. You people surprise me. I thought you would take a full pound of flesh."

They all walked out, Lambert holding the small machine gingerly, as if a sudden movement could erase the tape.

19

"I heard about Dominic," Roger said to Bunny. "Where the hell is he now?"

"He's okay. He collapsed somewhere, was taken to Oaktown General. And then checked out a few hours later. He left a message on my phone that he's okay."

They were standing on the spanking new floor of Budget Pharmacy. Behind them were four Wolves players—Turo, Loors, Ardmore, and Timken—uncomfortably dressed in suits and ties. In front of them was Julie Novick, in her wolf mascot outfit.

A man was walking around the store with a microphone, welcoming the league-leading Wolves to the store. It was, in fact, one of the biggest retail openings in years in Oaktown. Budget Pharmacy was really much more than a drugstore. It had three levels.

On the main level, where they all stood, was the drug department as well as shelf upon shelf

of toothpaste, aspirin, adhesive bandages, sham-
poos, disposable diapers—the entire monumental
panoply of bathroom supplies.

On the top level was budget clothing and fur-
niture. And on the bottom level were appliances
of all kinds, sporting goods, paints, hardware.

It was a downtown big-city store at its best—
gleaming, overstocked, with hundreds of signs
advertising elaborate sales, deals, coupon savings.

Bunny, Roger, and the players were there for
a price, but the team had always helped out in
retail and other promotions. It was part of the
myth, the mystique, that her father had started
many years ago, one that had fallen into abey-
ance while interim management had controlled
the team—but had been resurrected with a vengeance when Bunny took over the reins.

Near the players was a large aluminum folding
table, and on the table were dozens of brand-
new baseballs resting in small opened cartons.
The players were there to smile, to answer questions, and to sign and give away baseballs to
whoever wanted them as long as the supply
lasted.

Two photographers were snapping pictures.
Bunny had worn a demure skirt and blouse and
had pulled her long blond hair back and up
around her head. She looked like a Swedish
housewife. She smiled whenever she looked at the
Wolves players, because all of them, including
Roger, just didn't know how to dress. They always seemed to wear jackets and ties and shoes

that were at least three style changes old. They
always looked as if they had just emerged from
another generation.

She looked around for Tim Shea but then realized that he always tried to avoid these promotions at all costs, as most of the players did.
Usually they played "low card" in the locker
room to decide which of them would go and
which of them would receive a reprieve.

The customers began to gather around the
players and the table with the free baseballs. To
a great extent, they avoided the mascot because
they knew who was in the suit—Julie Novick—
and the papers had been full of articles about her
brother.

He had been portrayed as a rabid, psychotic
killer moving like a trained butcher through the
landscape. And yet, after all that time, the full
details of the murders had never been explicitly
revealed.

As for Julie, there was nothing she could do.
She had the feeling that she would soon lose the
job and the money that had been a godsend to
the Novick family. Her feelings for her brother
had now changed from fear to hatred. The
events—the suspicion—the newspaper publicity
that almost destroyed her mother. She spent the
entire day in an upstairs bedroom, in the dark,
praying for everyone. And in some odd sense her
mother had begun to blame Julie for the trouble;
as if Julie's lack of sisterly affection for Matt when
he had come home from jail was what drove her
poor son to do what he did. Her mother vacil-

lated between believing what they said about her
son and claiming that he was totally innocent and
would prove it the moment he decided to give
himself up.

Bunny was astonished by Julie Novick's courage; that she hadn't just resigned. Bunny realized
that sooner or later if the adverse publicity did
not calm down, she would have to dispense with
the mascot's services—but she was fighting
against that decision. The tragedy had nothing
to do with Julie; that her stolen wolf outfit might
be implicated or that her brother was in fact the
ghoulish killer was not her fault.

More customers were coming into the store
now, their shopping bags stuffed with opening-
day giveaways. In a small city like Oaktown,
which always had a substantial unemployment
problem, events like these drew a great many
people—particularly those out of work. They
were not raffish, just sad, and they wandered
around picking up free items and noting objects
they would purchase when times got better.

Roger said through clenched teeth, "God, I
hate these things."

"Learn to roll with it, Roger, learn to roll,"
said Bunny, laughing, accentuating the rolling
r's. She tapped him gently on the shoulder, in
consolation. She wondered why old baseball
players still seemed like children to her. She wondered why she felt that she had to take care of
Roger as well as Dominic, as well as the younger
players.

More customers surrounded the ballplayers and kept them busy.

"Look at Timken, he's in his glory," said Roger.

Bunny turned and stared at the short, squat catcher with the close-shaved red hair. He was in his catcher's crouch, demonstrating to a young boy and his mother how to get that quick release to cut down the runner attempting to steal second base.

"I like Timken," she said.

"Yeah," said Roger, "so do I."

A young woman materialized in front of them with a tray of coffee cups, and behind her another girl with stacks of small variously formed cakes. They each took a cup and a cake.

From where they stood they could see the brass band that was set up outside the store, and they could hear the marches being played.

"Where's our mascot?" Bunny asked, realizing that Julie Novick had vanished.

"I just saw her," Roger said, "by the table."

"She frightens people now. No one laughs at her antics," Bunny noted.

Roger chewed the piece of cake with a grimace, saying, "They baked this three days ago; it's like a stadium hot dog," and then looked for some place to dump it.

"Over there," said Bunny, trying to be helpful and pointing out a large wastebasket that obviously had been strategically placed for the celebration.

She pulled her pointing hand down quickly

when a woman stepped between them and the wastebasket.

The woman, whom Bunny did not know, seemed to be walking toward them.

She wore a brown cloth coat and a plastic rain hat, and she kept pulling at her eyeglasses with one hand.

She walked right up to Roger and whispered: "She's gone. I can't find her."

There was a dull sound in her voice. It was just a statement. Roger, uncomfortable, confused, looked at Bunny, who just shrugged her shoulders.

"She was with me a minute ago, and then she was gone," the woman said and she moved closer to Roger.

Then—suddenly—she screamed.

It was a scream so close and so loud and so pained that Bunny, immediately, involuntarily, covered her ears with her hands.

She's crazy, Bunny thought, she's crazy.

Then the woman ran toward Julie Novick in her mascot outfit, who had suddenly reappeared.

Julie seemed too shocked to move. The woman began to hit her and scream even louder.

Now Bunny could make out a child's name. Peggy. The woman was screaming about Peggy, who had vanished. Where was her daughter, Peggy?

Julie broke away from her and started to run toward the door of the store. Other customers stared—and then they began to throw things at Julie—at Julie in her wolf outfit—and there were screams of rage and fright. It seemed as if all the rumors and the fears and the reports had suddenly surfaced in one lethal uprising, blocking Julie's exit.

Then the ballplayers rushed to Julie and covered her with an umbrella of arms as bottles and packages and tubes clattered about them; as the frightened people, whipped into a frenzy by the screaming woman, tried to destroy the evil beast.

Then a man started forcing his way through the circle of people who blocked the front door.

He was holding a small child by the hand.

She was crying and smiling at the same time.

She saw the crazy woman and waddled over to her.

Then everyone realized that Peggy had been found . . . that Peggy was not dead . . . that Peggy was not mutilated . . . that the wolf was just a mascot.

No one knew what to do. Julie was cowering on the floor, having trouble breathing from the blows and the fear.

Bunny walked over to Roger and held his arm tightly. She could not say anything. She was trembling. For the first time since she had come home, that old hatred of Oaktown—the hatred she had as a young girl—had returned.

She wanted to go over to Julie and console her, but the mascot had become part of that hatred. She stared at the grotesque figure on the floor. Bunny felt herself going backward in time . . . to when she was a child . . . to the days when she was dragged to the stadium to see daddy's team play. It seemed that someone always commented on the ruthless way he had run the franchise. She felt so small, so insignificant, sitting in the special Bunsen box. Even though her father was dead, his presence was overpowering. He suffocated her. He suffocated everyone connected with the team. She wanted nothing but to escape.

Suddenly, the recollection faded. There was something unsettling about her childhood days at the ballpark—something evil that she still couldn't put her finger on.

20

THE four men stood around the desk in Roth's office at the south end of the detox ward. It was a small, cramped office, stuffed with journals and papers and two typewriters.

"If this is police work, I'll get out," said Roth, grinning. No matter what he said or how he said it, there was an essential gut friendliness about him that infected those around him.

"Stay," said Tournier. "You can help us to interpret alcoholics' language."

"Alcoholics don't have a language, they have a code."

Tournier sat down in Roth's chair. There was one other chair in the room. Dominic sat down in that one, his hand touching his leg slightly. He was obviously in pain.

"Turn it on and tune it up," Tournier said to Lambert. The detective flicked it on and then played with the volume.

"When you hear something that may be important, Dominic, just raise your hand and Lambert will stop it."

They listened in silence to Jackie Cannon's words. The speech was garbled, very garbled. In person his language at least sounded familiar, decipherable, as if it contained traditional words in traditional sentences. But now it was just gibberish.

Dominic raised a hand. Lambert shut it off.

"I think he mentioned the name of a guy who played on the 1963 team. I'm not sure, but it sounded like it." He nodded. Lambert turned it on again.

They all listened to the tape until it ended, without any further comments or interruptions.

"All clear?" asked Roth, amused.

"Did he know whom he was talking to? I mean, was he talking to someone?" Tournier asked Roth.

"I told you. The man is in the throes of the DT's. He is going through a great deal of convulsion, of random electrical discharges in the brain and the nervous system. I haven't the slightest idea if he knew whom he was talking to—much less what he was saying."

"You mean he could have been singing a nonsense song, and we're making asses of ourselves trying to make sense out of it."

"Exactly," Roth responded.

Tournier noticed that Dominic wasn't really listening to them. His hands were folded on his lap and he was staring straight ahead.

"Did you hear anything?" he asked Dominic.

The older man didn't respond. He didn't mention the names of the 1963 ballplayers he thought he had heard when they were in the cell-like room. He unfolded his hands and ran them through his thick, bristled gray hair.

Finally, Dominic spoke, but to Roth: "You have to fix that poor bastard up. Isn't there anything you can do for him?"

"He'll come out of it," Roth said.

"I mean now," Dominic shouted.

"No, not now. We're doing all we can. Do I have to go through that textbook stuff again with you people? That man—your friend or your suspect or whatever the hell he is to you—is in a medical emergency. I shouldn't even have let you bother him."

"You don't understand," Dominic said in a careful, almost dangerous voice. "We don't have time."

Roth shrugged and smiled.

"Well," Tournier interrupted, "I heard something."

"Yeah, gibberish," Lambert retorted wearily.

"No. Play it again," Tournier said.

The tape went on again. While it was playing, Tournier scrambled around the desk in front of him until he found a pencil and paper. Then he waited and listened. Three quarters of the way through he said, softly: "It's coming up soon."

They all moved closer to the tape recorder.

And they heard something strange, less garbled, but not coherent enough to hang their hat on. Perhaps it was a foreign language.

They watched Tournier write. And then the tape ended.

They gathered around the table and stared at the transcription.

It read: "NITINATSHAMANCALSPRTOME."

"Maybe it's his Indian language."

"Cannon's an Indian?"

"Part Indian," Dominic said.

"It's nonsense," Lambert said.

"It's the only phrase or group of phrases that he said that could be heard clearly," Tournier noted. "It was as if he had slowed down. As if he were talking to us. I put it down syllable by syllable."

"Wait a minute," Roth said, the smile finally vanishing from his face. "What kind of Indian?"

"I don't know. Some kind of American Indian. From around the Coast, Vancouver Island, maybe," Dominic answered.

"Well, well, well," said Roth, suddenly excited, grabbing the pencil from Tournier.

"I collect Indian masks," he said, and placed a mark on the page, separating the first seven letters from the rest of the line that Tournier had transcribed. "And," he added with a flourish, "among the tribes which were the finest artists in wood, were the NITINAT."

"You mean there is a tribe of Indians called the Nitinat?"

"Not really a tribe. Let's call them a differentiated group within a larger language grouping of Indians that speak a language called Nootkan.

Great whalers all of them, at one time. Great artists all of them."

"Then the word after that is clear now," said Tournier, picking up the excitement of the chase. "SHAMAN."

"Exactly—a witch doctor. The Coast tribes were famous for the power and prestige of their shamans."

They were left with the last eleven letters.

"Look," said Roth, finally pulling his glasses down over his eyes, "he was telescoping his words like drunks do. S-P-R-T is really SPIRIT. You see?"

Lambert leaped in. "And the chief just left out the H in front of OME."

"So what do we have?" Tournier asked.

"The Nitinat shaman is calling or called the spirit home."

"What the hell does that mean?"

"I don't know," Roth said.

Tournier leaned back into the chair and closed his eyes. Nothing was falling into place. Nothing was bringing them closer.

When he opened his eyes he saw Dominic hovering over him, like a hungry hawk.

"I remember something else," the old man said.

"About what?"

"That word—*Nitinat*."

"It's a tribe of Indians, Dominic."

"I remember the word."

"Pertaining to what?"

"To 1963."

Tournier sighed. He had begun to accept Dominic's feeling that 1963 was somehow related to the horror . . . that the 1963 baseball championship had, as the drunk said, won them death. Whatever that meant. But now, in the weary aftermath of the Cannon interview, it seemed merely like the ramblings of an old man.

"What was the name of that girl again? The one in the parochial school?"

"Joanne Swift."

"And her grandfather?"

"Louis Swift. He was director of public works years ago. You said he was a drinking buddy of Walter Bunsen's."

"Yes, he was," Dominic said, smacking the table with one twisted catcher's hand. "He was director of public works in 1963, and there was a hell of a row about him."

"When?"

"In 1963."

"About what?"

"About a Nitinat girl."

"About what?"

"About an Indian girl who was killed."

"Murdered?"

"No. An accident."

Dominic spun around and began to pace along the far wall, banging into stacks of magazines and hurting his leg again. Roth pulled the chair over so he could sit.

"Go slow, Dominic, go slow. Talk it out," Tournier said.

"My memory is not very clear. But I remember

there was an accident. An Indian girl died. She somehow was buried in the town dump. She fell into it . . . or something like that."

"What else?"

"There was this investigation or something. Anyway, the body was never found. They sealed the dump. It was never used again. It's still there, north of the Armory District, on County Road 11."

"I know it. I used to play around there as a kid," Lambert said.

"What was the girl's name?" Tournier asked.

Dominic began to pace again in that strange fashion of his, with the gimpy leg, his face contorted with the twin effort of trying to recall the past and trying to walk with two legs in the present.

"I don't remember the goddamn name. I just remember she vanished. They closed the dump. The whole mess was right before the 1963 season."

"But she was Indian?"

"Right."

"If you can't remember her name, Dominic, how in hell can you remember that she was a Nitinat Indian?"

"I don't know why. But I remember the Indian name Nitinat. I remember that the girl was described that way."

"What kind of accident was it?"

"I don't remember. A car or a bus, maybe."

Tournier stared out the doctor's window. The thought came to him suddenly that Dominic might be as mad as Jackie Cannon—that Dominic saw everything through a baseball lens; that he remembered years not by world events or personal events but by which team had won the pennant in which league. The year 1963 had begun to balloon, to expand in both Cannon's and Dominic's minds. It had begun to reach out and grab all their imaginations—but it might be total nonsense; the paranoid visions of an arthritic ex-catcher and an alcoholic. That he, Tournier, was now listening to and following the thought processes of two old ballplayers was a tribute to the trap that he had gotten himself into. There were still few clues. There were still no explanations. Murder and mutilation were somehow more bearable if you knew how and why. If you did not, then the act tore you apart as it had torn the victims.

Above all, he knew that one could not live rationally in the face of such horror without an explanation. One could not simply continue living as usual from day to day—getting up, washing, eating, going to sleep.

Tournier stared around the room and grinned: it was insane—two high-powered cops and a physician listening to an old crazed baseball player, while down the hall there was an alky with the DT's whose every word was treated like a mathematical formula of great importance.

God help us, Tournier thought, and Dominic most of all.

Dominic picked up on Tournier's growing skepticism. The old man kept silent. He wished

he was among baseball people; he wished right
then he was with Roger and Bunny or anyone
who was connected to the team. Maybe it was
only a game, a silly game, but at least it taught
people how to think clearly.

You stepped into the batter's box with a piece
of wood in your hands. You stared at a pitcher
who was throwing a horsehide ball ninety miles
an hour in your direction from a distance of sixty
feet. You had to adjust your body and your piece
of wood to make contact with the hurtling
sphere. You had to think. You had to react. Goddamn Tournier was not thinking, not reacting.
He didn't even believe the incident by the freight
cars. He didn't share the horror that he, Dominic, had sensed behind him; that dancing malev-
olent beast—sightless, nameless.

Yes, Tournier thought Dominic should have
turned around and faced it—if it was truly there.
Only then would Tournier have believed him or
understood what Jackie Cannon had said. And
even now, when Roth had deciphered that
strange gobbledygook, Dominic knew that Tournier didn't believe the threat of 1963—he didn't
believe that it was somehow, in some manner,
all connected.

Dominic suddenly grew very sad; what would
happen if it struck again . . . ? Oh God, what
would happen if there was another Larrabee . . .
a human creature gutted like a piece of lawn . . .
the insides scooped out.

"The *Oaktown Logger* keeps files," Lambert
said. He was talking about the daily newspaper,

which had been in continuous publication for almost ninety years.

"Why not?" Tournier asked no one in particular, and without enthusiasm. Then he turned to Roth and said: "I appreciate the help you have given us."

21

OAKTOWN, the city itself, was beginning to reel from the effects of the horror. The sick jokes had begun.

There were jokes about the dangers of going into bathrooms. There were jokes about how to put bodies together after they had been ripped apart.

One particularly demented person had left carefully wrapped chicken parts—the head wrapped in tinfoil, the wings in plastic, the legs in Xmas paper—in front of City Hall, Cathedral School, and one of the local churches with a note pinned on. "Guess Who?" it said.

One jokester had invented a game: "Assemble the Parts." It was a board game. You rolled the dice and it came up leg or thigh or breast or tongue. And the one who assembled a corpse first won. Of course there were some rolls of the dice that brought forth a mutilated part, which had to be discarded, and the player then lost points.

But it was not all this black humor that disturbed Bunny as she sat with Tim Shea in a car overlooking the Japanese-style pagoda that guarded the entrance to a state park twenty miles outside the city limits of Oaktown. They often came to this place when they wanted to be alone without making love—just to talk . . . just to spend some peaceful time together.

And it wasn't the idiotic attack on Julie Novick in the drugstore that disturbed her either; she could understand a mother suddenly losing sight of a child and acting in a deranged manner.

No—what really disturbed her was that no one seemed to be in control any longer. No one knew who or what was out there. No one seemed even close to finding out. Matt Novick was fast becoming a mythic character; if he did exist and if they could find him . . . if . . . if . . .

The strands that seemed to hold together different factions in a city were beginning to unravel. She could feel it. She could feel it in the stadium where, for the first time since she had taken over the team, there had been a bloody fight in the bleachers with racial overtones.

Even her lover, Tim Shea, was becoming disturbed.

He had just told her, as they sat in the car, that he'd had a dream about Larrabee.

"Do you remember it?" she asked, tousling his hair as if he were a kid and moving closer to him so that their flanks were pressed against each other.

"Parts of it," Tim said, and she had never

heard his voice so strained. "Larrabee kept on losing limbs. I mean, he was talking to me and his hand would vanish and he would joke about it, but I didn't think it was a joke—and each time another part of his body vanished, I felt sicker. And then I woke up."

"Larrabee wasn't ripped apart like the young girl," she said.

"Right. So you say. But who the hell knows what really happened to Larrabee? Who the hell cares?"

Perhaps, she thought, dreams were sweeping the city; everyone was having nightmares. Perhaps this human or this beast or this force was seeping into their collective unconscious—like a psychic oil stain.

She, herself, had had a nightmare two nights before, but she could not tell it to anyone; it was too ugly and too private. Even in the car, remembering it, she felt such a distaste, such an almost clinical horror, that she shook her head vigorously.

"What's the matter?" Tim asked, kissing her on the neck.

"Nothing."

Tim placed both hands on the wheel. She stared at his hands; they were nice, strong, but not bulky. She liked baseball players' hands; they were out of the ordinary. They had to be quick and powerful and incredibly sensitive—all at the same time.

"I got a feeling we may go all the way this year," Tim said.

"Because you had one good save?" she chided him. He bit her neck playfully in return.

"I think," he whispered, "I am beginning to fall in love with you."

"Why whisper?" she asked. "We're twenty miles away from the nearest soul."

She stared down at the Japanese-style pagoda. She remembered a paper she once wrote about Oscar Wilde in a college literature course. Wilde had written about the magnificent medieval Japanese painters whose images of Japan were what Westerners saw, then and now . . . it was their paintings that defined the spirit of Japan for generations of Americans, British, French. Wilde had noted that while the brush strokes were beautiful and true in one sense, they had absolutely nothing to do with the real world. For as Wilde said, "There is no such country. There are no such people." In other words, if you went to Japan you'd see only a few farms, a few factories, a few of everything, but none of that exquisite subtlety.

That was her mistake also. She was trying to create a city, a people, by means of a baseball team. All the beauty and color and grace and speed of the Oaktown Wolves would somehow be transferred to the community. A pipedream.

Suddenly, she grabbed one of Tim's hands and pressed it against her sweater. Then she slipped it under her sweater onto her naked breast. His hand was cold. She wanted him to press hard, to hurt her.

She felt for some reason as though she were

hundreds of miles away from Oaktown. But at the same time she felt she could visualize what was taking place there—right now. How people were beginning to scurry, as the shadows lengthened. How people were beginning to act like rodents, to start at a single sound and scrunch their bodies up; to sniff the air because danger was close, always so close; to keep with them weapons that could break the onslaught of an attack of teeth and claws—if that was what they were.

"I think, Timmy," she said, "you love everyone you sleep with."

22

ON the way out they stopped at the small window cut into the door of the room where Jackie Cannon was being held in full sheet restraint.

Dominic stared inside. Jackie was now lying on his side, his face pressed against the slick floor. It was as if he were there for the calmness of the floor, its grain, its cleanliness, to soothe him.

"When does he get out of that stupid thing?" Dominic asked Roth.

"Soon, very soon," Roth responded.

Dominic gave Roth a withering look, as if to suggest the younger man was not much of a physician if he had to use full sheet restraint to treat alkies. Then he stared back into the room. He wanted to communicate somehow to Jackie Cannon that he understood the importance of Jackie's information. He didn't understand what the words meant—about the shaman calling the spirits home—but he knew that Jackie was trying to help, was trying to convey the whole story of what he had hinted at before. Dominic wanted somehow to let Jackie Cannon know that only a fool would not believe he spoke the truth; that he knew things no one else did; that he knew why they had all won death in its most hideous form.

Dominic had the weirdest impulse as he stared through the small window: he wanted to give Jackie a baseball glove or a bat. He just wanted to go inside and lay the stuff beside him. But he didn't have a glove or a bat. And the door was locked in front of him.

"Let's get moving," said Tournier, and the three exited the building, leaving Roth at the door.

Lambert drove fast, without the siren, and on the brake, keeping to the edges of the road as if, once threatened by another car, he would happily ride up on the sidewalk. No one bothered him; the unmarked cars of the Oaktown police force were even more conspicuous than the marked cars. Dominic counted the number of lights Lambert ran—four.

He heard Tournier, who was seated in the front beside Lambert, mumble several times. At first Dominic thought Tournier was chastising Lambert for the wild ride, but then he moved forward in the back seat and heard familiar words—Tournier was repeating the phrase they had deciphered—"The Nitinat shaman is calling the spirits home." He was reciting it as if it were a television ditty; an advertisement for a show. Then Dominic realized that was not quite it. The police chief was trying to memorize the phrase in various ways, to turn it over on his tongue, as if he were absorbing and discarding signals from a third-base coach in that age-old ritual of cooperation and deception on the baseball diamond. Dominic leaned back in his seat again and kept his feet planted against the bottom of the front seat for support during Lambert's sweeping turns.

The *Oaktown Logger* was situated in a squat, ugly building right behind the city's administration building, which held all the elected and many of the appointed municipal officers except for the mayor, who was in City Hall, and the judges, who were in the courthouse, and the police and fire departments, which had their own buildings.

While the *Logger* was now a high-tech paper with terminals instead of typewriters and scanning devices instead of ink, the backfile was maintained in a completely nineteenth-century fashion of gentlemanly disarray.

A small woman in a red dress told them that there was only one copy of each paper for each date, that there were no microfilm or microfiche copies, that there was no subject index.

Each copy was preserved in a large waxed envelope and stacked according to day.

"We need all of 1963 because we have really no idea when the child died, except that it was in 1963," Tournier explained, ignoring Dominic's earlier comment that the child had definitely died shortly before the 1963 baseball season commenced.

The woman arched her eyebrows. "That's about three hundred and fifty days' worth of newspapers."

"So it is," Tournier agreed.

She moved away from her chair and motioned for them to follow her. Into the stacks they went, and she pointed out the perimeters of their search. They thanked her. Tournier told Lambert to start at the beginning of the year. He and Dominic would start at the end of 1963 and work their way backward.

It was Lambert who found the information about twenty minutes later. The incident had been reported in February—on the seventh, eighth, and ninth. That was, indeed, as Dominic said, before the baseball season commenced, way before.

The three men hovered around the tables on which the back issues were spread out and pieced together what had happened from the reports.

On the afternoon of February 6, a Volkswagen bus, carrying several Indian children and their parents from a visit to relatives east of Oaktown, stopped off on the side of the road to let the passengers eat, stretch, and rest before continuing their drive to the Coast.

One of the girls, Patricia Highsmith, eleven years old, wandered off.

She did not come back.

They looked for her and discovered, to their horror, that they had parked right next to the steep, swampy end of the town dump, and only a few steps from their vehicle was a very steep incline, almost a free-fall, into the swamp.

The child was not found. There was some evidence that she had fallen down the slope and been sucked into the swamp: scratch marks on the dirt and one of her hair ribbons.

The Indians asked the city to excavate the swamp—to drain it as much as possible until the child's body was found. The Commissioner of Public Works, Louis Swift, said he was not empowered by the charter to do that.

There were demonstrations, threats, lawsuits. But the upshot was, the girl was never found; the swampy end of the town dump was never drained.

In fact, it was the Patricia Highsmith incident that really closed and sealed the dump; the city hired a private carting service and a private landfill shortly thereafter.

"Notice," Tournier said, "they mention a dozen times that the girl was Indian, that the people in the van were Indians, but the reporter never identifies the tribe."

"Maybe he never asked," Lambert replied.

"Are you finished?" Dominic asked Lambert.

The detective nodded and pushed all the papers toward Dominic, who wanted to read them close up because his eyes were bad.

He read all the relevant articles carefully. There was no mention of Walter Bunsen or the Oaktown Wolves. There was no mention of the 1963 team—but how could there be? The season hadn't started yet.

23

ROTH, whose first name was Felix, but whom everyone called Max, spent some time with Jackie Cannon after the three visitors had left.

The fact that Jackie Cannon had turned out to be one half Coast Indian made him even more solicitous of the man than he had been before he knew. Roth had always been fascinated by those Indians. Growing up on the West Side of Manhattan, he had spent half his days in the bowels of the American Museum of Natural History, which held astonishing re-creations of their way of life, their long boats, their weapons, their fierce art, their potlaches.

They had, in fact, formed his fantasy life for many years, and they were one of the main reasons he had migrated to the Pacific Coast.

As for ending up as a staff physician at an alcoholism treatment center, he made no excuses for that, even though it was considered one of the least lucrative and least appreciated of all possible medical careers. Alcoholism was at the very core of American society, he knew; it was the number one disease in terms of morbidity and fatality. Probably half the beds in all psychiatric and general hospitals were filled by individuals who were alcoholic but not diagnosed as such.

And he liked treating them. He liked detoxing them; he liked helping them; he liked seeing them sober.

Jackie Cannon was doing okay, he thought, as he squatted by the restrained man and talked to him gently. The crisis would be over soon, and he could go back to the regular ward.

From now on it would be cookbook stuff— some tranquilizers to keep his anxiety level down, some exercise, some group therapy . . . and vitamin and trace element supplementation along with many high protein/low carbohydrate meals each day to get his hypoglycemia under control and reverse the systemic malnourishment that was always present in hard-core alcoholics like Cannon.

He walked back to his small cluttered office and sat down, exhausted. Those three men had worn him out, but the deciperment of Cannon's alcoholic gibberish continued to intrigue him.

In fact, he knew very little about the Coast Indians in spite of his romantic love for them. He had always wanted to begin a comprehensive study of their customs as they existed before the white men destroyed them—but he ended up only collecting their art, particularly their masks.

Even that endeavor had become too expensive over the past few years.

The deciphered phrase had nudged some memory. What was it? "The Nitinat shaman is calling the spirits home."

Something about the phrase was familiar. Something about it was very familiar. He really didn't give a damn about their bizarre police procedures, or the murders—there was nothing he could do about that or them. But his basic intellectual curiosity was challenged.

He got up from his chair and waded through the unread journals and books until he reached the back of the bookcase where he kept his books on Indian art. But he wasn't looking for the monographs, which, for the most part, had been published by museums or university presses. He was looking for an encyclopedic work on the Pacific Coast Indians that he had purchased many years ago on a trip to San Francisco.

When he found the book, buried under a stack of magazines on American Indian art with auction prices, he discovered that there was no entry for the Nitinats.

He had forgotten that the usual classification in a reference work about American Indians was by language.

Roth looked up the entry for Nootkan, which ran seventy-one closely printed pages with hundreds of illustrations.

Then he found what he had been looking for, what he had remembered vaguely before: that the main ceremony of the Nootkan-speaking peoples was the Dancing Society.

In English it was called the Wolf Dance, because the main spirits represented were those of wolves.

In the Nootkan language, the name of the performance means "the Shamans"!

The connection was even more precise than he had realized when they deciphered Cannon's gibberish.

It was an exact parallel. Cannon had said that the shaman was calling the spirits home.

That, in fact, was what the Wolf Dance was all about.

Mutilation. Dismemberment. A savage and brutal murder. No clues. A demon loosed.

All that he had heard over the last few weeks was on that thin line between the rational and the irrational.

Even grown, intelligent people were beginning to become frightened, to speculate that there was a beast out there who could not be classified; who could not be trapped; who could not be understood.

He had remembered the ceremony itself, but not the particulars. He read on.

"In ancient times an ancestor entered the supernatural House of the Wolves, where the Wolf Spirits dwelt in human form. The wolves gave him wisdom, taught him songs and dances to take back to his people. After four days of instruction they brought him back to his village where he discovered that he had been away for four years.

He taught his village what the spirits had taught him and instructed them how to rescue him from the wolves. This is the central myth of the Nootkan-speaking Indians.

"In the ceremony, musical instruments represent the howling of the wolf spirits. The wolf spirits kidnap young children, novices. The village rescues the kidnapped children, who have been held captive in canoes. The children who are rescued paint their faces and dance with the supernatural power that they received from the wolf spirits. They sing songs they have learned among the wolves and announce their new names, which the wolves have given them. All children of the Nootkan-speaking tribes participate in this dance at least once prior to adolescence—they are all taken by the wolf spirits."

Roth stopped reading. What an astonishing fit.

A drunk talks gibberish. A cop deciphers it. A city is paralyzed by a lunatic. A doctor finds a description that relates to the decipherment.

He took the book and walked slowly to his desk, sitting down wearily. The excitement had passed. He remembered that the three visitors were going to the newspaper—the *Oaktown Logger*. He called there.

24

THE only thing about the whole bizarre explanation that Dominic found at all plausible was the dancing part. He had heard the thing dance; he had sensed the thing dancing.

Tournier, Dominic, Lambert, Roth, and Bunny were seated in the *Logger*'s library. The small woman in the red dress had long since gone. Each of them held a Xerox copy of what Roth had found in the book.

Tournier had asked Dominic to call Bunny; to get her there so that she was in on all the latest information. Tournier had carefully described to her what they had discovered in the detox ward; what Jackie Cannon had told them.

"I think, finally, we have some idea of what is going on—what we might be facing."

"I don't see how we know anything," Dominic said, staring for a moment at Dr. Roth.

"We know a lot. We know that all of the victims have been mutilated in some way, and it could be said that the mutilations were wolflike. We know that in 1963 an Indian child was killed in an accident in the town dump. We know that two of the victims were near her age. We know that the girl's tribe worshipped and danced to wolf spirits."

"So what? What about Larrabee? Larrabee was a grown man. You got it all wrong. The connection is with the baseball team—with the Wolves."

Dominic stopped. He didn't want to continue the conversation because he knew that Tournier didn't believe he was almost attacked that night by the abandoned freight terminal.

"Do we forget about Matt Novick?" Lambert asked. His question was ignored.

Tournier spun out a theory: "It appears to me that we are looking for an Indian, a member of the Nitinat or some Nootkan-speaking people, who is acting out a large revenge drama of his own. Who, through lunacy or booze or drugs, is doing this wolf dance in our city . . . only this time the dance is for real. Maybe by killing these girls he is somehow, in his demented brain, trying to ransom the Indian girl. Maybe he believes the Indian girl is not in the sealed-over dump, but is instead a hostage to the wolf spirits in their lair."

"One could imagine hundreds of scenarios," Roth said, smiling at Bunny, whom he had heard of but never met—and whom he found most attractive.

"Yes, well, there may be a hundred scenarios,

but there is probably only one murderer. Do you people agree with my assessment? An Indian, deranged most likely, acting out some kind of cosmic drama of redemption for a dead girl whose body the city of Oaktown was either never willing or never able to recover and return."

"I don't know what to say," Bunny responded. "I just got here. The whole thing sounds crazy."

Tournier looked around. He was patient. He understood that there would be skepticism. He understood that he was a step ahead of them because of his training, and he would have to carefully lay out what was known. The developments of the past few hours had brought Tournier great relief. He could stand any kind of crime, any kind of horror, any kind of explanation of an event—as long as it was rational. That was what had been missing in all the murders. He had reluctantly been drawn into a mystical, almost a supernatural net that elicited only fear and confusion.

Now the real world had saved them all—as horrible as it was.

Roth asked: "You don't need me anymore, do you?"

Tournier replied: "Look, I want to thank you very much. You were extremely helpful. You gave us what we need. But, if it is not too much trouble, I would appreciate your hanging around a little longer. Can you do that?"

Roth thought for a while, agreed, and then excused himself to make some phone calls. He was back at the table in five minutes. No one had spoken. No one had left.

When he came back, Lambert made some calls for food and coffee—which was brought in.

Finally, when they were all reseated at the table, their sandwiches and coffee containers opened in front of them, Tournier asked: "What do we do now?"

Lambert answered: "Flush him out."

Tournier responded: "Exactly. But how?"

Dominic picked up his sandwich and examined what was between the pieces of bread. He had asked for a ham and cheese; this was what it was, but it was the real cheap ham, which he hated, the kind he used to get instead of bologna sandwiches when he had first started in baseball more than half a century ago . . . when you got a dollar a day for meal money.

"I think I know how," Tournier said. The chief of police of the city of Oaktown reached across the table and tapped the copy of the paper that contained Patricia Highsmith's photo the day after her death.

"It is," he continued, "the twenty-fifth anniversary of the accident. Let's have a memorial service for the girl at the site."

Tournier waited for a response. He heard none, but noted interest. They were sipping their coffee and staring at him.

He continued: "We do it quickly. Tomorrow evening. We announce it on the radio and in the papers, but no further publicity. People will ignore it. Our friend may not. We don't need any-

thing for the ceremony except a few musicians.
And a plaque. We'll place down a plaque hon-
oring her memory."

"The Indians would view something like this
as a profound desecration."

"Exactly," agreed Tournier, "so that if the lunatic is still around, if in his demented brain he
is somehow gathering the kidnapped from the
wolf spirits, he'll come for us. He'll stop it. He'll
hurt us. He has to."

Dominic nodded his head. He thought Tournier was way off base, but the idea was a good
one—simple, quick; you'd know one way or the
other almost immediately.

"Bunny, can you get the musicians for us? The
same ones you use for the stadium? And a few
members of the team?"

"Sure," Bunny said, "and I'll ask Roger and
maybe Tim Shea to come along."

Dominic grinned into his coffee. It was the first
time Bunny had slipped up like that and mentioned Tim Shea in one of her conversations
without any qualifying disclaimers—such as, he
was a lousy relief pitcher. Maybe she's getting
serious with him, Dominic conjectured. What the
hell—she was old enough.

"What about Jackie Cannon? Can you get him
there?" Tournier asked Roth.

"No way," Roth said, "except on a stretcher."

"Then forget it," Tournier responded, "just a
thought. Now here's the way it'll look." He
waited until he had their complete attention and

said: "We'll park the cars just off the main road. Then walk down the shallow north incline."

"The girl died on the other side of the dump."

"I know, but it's too steep there. We couldn't handle it," Tournier responded, waited for further objections, and when there were none, continued. "We have two of those large searchlights out there on the flat truck; the band plays a bit; one of us or the preacher makes a speech; and then we unveil the plaque. Simple and quick. If something happens, it happens. If nothing happens, we go home."

"What preacher?" Dominic asked.

"Why a preacher?" Roth asked. "Why not just someone representing the city . . . the city's way of asking forgiveness for not finding the child originally."

"You're right."

"Why not you, Chief?" Roth asked.

"You're right again. Why not me?"

Tournier turned to Lambert to get confirmation, but Lambert was busy scribbling on his pad. Tournier felt good—Lambert was on the ball, and when he was, things got done. He could visualize the list on the pad: get plaque made up; contact radio station and paper about ceremony; reserve flatbed truck with searchlights; check out area in A.M.

"Let's make it tomorrow evening at nine," Tournier suggested. He looked around the table. There were no objections.

"And let's make it a procession," he added.

"What do you mean by a procession?" Bunny asked.

"We'll all meet about eight-thirty in front of the police station. We'll all go out together in a couple of cars and the flatbed truck will follow. It's more formal that way. It's more like a real event."

"But if you're putting a plaque down, it is a real event," Roth noted.

"Like Jackie Cannon's real event," Dominic interjected bitterly, letting Roth know that he was still disturbed by Cannon's treatment; by the full sheet restraint that Roth claimed was needed to keep him from hurting himself or others during the DT convulsions.

It was settled. It would be done. One by one they left, until only Dominic remained at the long table, strewn with paper bags and half-eaten sandwiches and paper cups.

He felt numb. He felt as if his body had given up. There was a very slight throbbing in his head; like a pulse.

He stared at the debris of the table—the bread, the meat, the slivers of pickle, the small cups of cole slaw with the slaw running over the sides, half-drunk coffee containers, torn sugar packets, tiny milk containers, crumpled napkins.

Dominic was not a religious man. He had lapsed as a Catholic in his early twenties. But sitting there, right then, he believed there was surely a God in heaven and that God would judge. The sudden intuition made him afraid. He slipped down into his chair. He felt that somehow God was judging him right then. He felt that God knew his entire life, his entire mind, that God was aware of every single tiny sin he had ever committed.

His chest began to pound. He felt his neck stiffen. He wanted to flee but couldn't.

He blinked his eyes furiously. Something was happening to the leftover food on the table.

He stared at half an uneaten sandwich. It was changing. He could not make it out yet—not yet.

His legs were trembling.

He was watching the young girl's throat, torn from the body.

The sweat poured out from his forehead and upper lip.

Other things changed. Scattered up and down the table he saw the bloody remnants of all the murders—he saw the remnants that had vanished; the throat, the viscera. He saw the parts of the schoolgirl's body, reproduced exactly.

I am going to die, he thought. I am going to die now and be judged. That is why I am going insane.

Gathering all his strength, he flung himself off the chair and slammed hard against the table. The pain was excruciating. He fell to the floor and rolled over. He lay there, silent, afraid to move. Finally, he rolled over again and fearfully, painfully, he rose, peering at the top of the table.

The leftovers had become leftovers again. All that was there were cole slaw containers and half-eaten sandwiches and empty cardboard containers that were rolling back and forth from one end of the table to another like a cosmic pinball game. I was having an hallucination, he thought. He placed his arms on the table, lay his head down on them, and he rested.

25

THERE were seven musicians. They were playing an old hymn: "Hear Us When We Pray to Thee for Those in Peril on the Sea." A damp, cool wind swirled about them, stifling the sounds.

The powerful lights illuminated large circles on the filthy, overgrown, and abandoned dump. They shone from the road, from the flatbed truck on which they were perched.

While the music played, they all watched as Lambert cleared a small patch of ground with a shovel. It was hard work. Layers of windblown dirt and shrubs covered the dump, but when the surface was broken a myriad of garbage began to emerge. It was like entering a secret world.

Behind Lambert was Tournier, holding a plaque mounted on a piece of stone. It would be placed onto the ground after Lambert was through.

Behind Tournier were Bunny and Tim Shea and Roger, and a bit behind him were Dominic and Roth. As the music played, as Lambert dug, Roth whispered to Dominic: "Who's crazier? Us or the one we've set the trap for?"

Dominic didn't answer. He felt very uncomfortable standing there. Sure there were two large beams of light, but beyond the beams and for miles in each direction was only abandoned darkness.

The dump gave off a strange smell, so pungent that it seemed to enter one's clothes, one's shoes, one's head.

"I mean," continued Roth to Dominic, "is this gentleman going to show up in his tribal outfit or in a sports coat?"

Dominic just grinned at the physician's humor. Then he moved away from him a bit, toward Bunny and Shea and Roger, toward the baseball people.

Lambert was almost finished creating a flat, appropriate spot for the memorial. He flung bits of debris that he dug up back into the darkness.

The musicians had finished the hymn. Next they played a somewhat rousing march. It was beginning to get chilly and damp.

The twin lights from the flatbed truck pierced the darkness with less force, and if one studied the light from the side, moisture hung on the beams.

Finally Lambert stepped back. All those gathered could see the space—flat, perfect.

Lambert walked over to Tournier, who handed the memorial to him, and the detective placed it down on the ground, then stood on it with all his weight to plant it firmly; then he stepped off and carefully wiped all dirt from the memorial.

When Tournier stepped forward, the mood of the assemblage changed. It had been a flippant mood because they were setting a trap for a madman, and so it really was a scam. The memorial to the Indian girl was a scam. And because it was a scam Tournier's words would be meaningless. No one there knew the girl. No one there remembered the girl. No one there lost any kind of sleep over her death at the time it happened, twenty-five years ago, or during any of the subsequent years.

But when Tournier stepped forward to deliver his address, the flippancy died; the assembled realized that the girl was there, underneath them somewhere, perhaps under their very feet. She had been lost in the dump—right there. The body had never been found. It was possible that she, it, would suddenly erupt from the ground, just like the old toaster or the twisted pieces of plastic or the car door.

Dominic was not fidgety. It was like one of those innumerable old-timers' games he had attended where there were always ridiculous speeches tied into genuine sentiment for the dead and those about to be dead.

Tournier began to speak, reading with difficulty from a small sheaf of notes. He twisted his body to let the arc light shine more squarely on the paper.

He said: "We are here to memorialize a tragic death. Twenty-five years is a long time to wait to right a wrong. We hope that our presence here will do justice to this child's memory."

He turned the page over and was about to continue when the night was split by a massive screeching of automobile gears, the sound of brakes squealing against wet macadam, and then a quick, dull thud.

The onlookers turned away from Tournier and began to race up the slope to the road.

Some tripped, some fell, and two or three of the band members fell down with their instruments.

When they reached the road, smoke and small darts of fire were coming from a red pickup truck that had slammed into the back of the flatbed truck.

"Get an extinguisher," Tournier yelled to Lambert.

They pulled the driver out of the vehicle. He was dazed but able to walk. One side of his face was bruised.

Roth inspected the man carefully while the fire was put out.

"He's okay," the physician said, noting to Tournier that the man had been drinking.

"What else is new?"

When the fire was extinguished they all helped to push the vehicle onto the shoulder on the far side of the road.

The driver was helped into the cab of the flatbed truck and covered with a blanket just in case. Roth said there was no need for hospitalization, and they decided to drop him off at the

Oaktown General emergency ward just after the ceremony was over.

"Lucky those lights are still functioning after the impact," Lambert said. And they were functioning well, sending out the dual beams, the spotlights onto the dump.

They all began to return to the scene of the memorial. Halfway there, their feet crunching on the strange feel of the covered-over dump, Dominic asked: "Where the hell is Roger?"

They waited for him. He was not on the road. He was not in the flatbed truck. He was not anywhere on the slope.

Dominic yelled out his name. There was no answer.

Dominic turned away from the road. He saw something on the small memorial stone, the plaque, that Lambert had placed there.

He walked quickly to it.

"My God," Roth whispered behind him.

Lying on the slab were two blue-gray eyes— Roger's eyes—ripped out of their sockets and dribbling over the memorial.

Dominic felt his legs turn to jelly and he reached out for someone—anyone.

26

THEY entered Texas before it was light. Rowse was driving their latest car—a 1983 yellow Ford Mustang they had stolen out of a motel parking lot, leaving in its place an old blue Pontiac Firebird, also stolen, as were the five prior vehicles that had been used and "traded."

Matt Novick sat next to the driver. He was pale, tired, and on edge. He was counting money—tens, twenties.

"How much we got?" Rowse asked.

"Looks like nine hundred dollars left."

"Hell," said Rowse, "we can get a long way on that."

Matt put a thick rubber band around the bills and flung the package up on the dashboard.

As he sat back he caught a glimpse of Chico, asleep in the back seat. Chico was obviously a nut. All he did was drink beer and sleep. He never talked. He probably couldn't speak English. But he was brave, very brave. And he obviously didn't care about anything or anyone, particularly himself.

As for Rowse, well, he was a typical lunatic biker—tattooed speed. He had dragons on his thighs, a falcon over each breast, mystical signs tattooed on three fingers of each hand—and he popped little green pills from the time he got up to the time he went to sleep. But, in fact, he rarely slept.

It was Rowse who really knew what to do. When they ran out of money he pointed out a gas station or a store.

When it was time to change cars, Rowse was the one who would find a new one fast. Rowse knew when to travel and when to lay low. And Rowse was the one who had gotten the weapons . . . he knew where to buy guns and ammo wherever they were.

Now they had three pieces—one S and W .38, one 9mm semiautomatic, and one sawed-off shotgun.

They were moving along the flat West Texas terrain at about seventy-five miles an hour. Dawn was approaching. Strange slivers of half light surrounded the car. The road was deserted, empty. Matt Novick had never been this far east in his life.

He closed his eyes and let the breeze from the open window play against his face. He couldn't get far enough away from Oaktown. He would never go back. He would never give up. He would drive until they caught him and blew him away. That was the way it would have to be.

Too much had gone down. Too many robberies.
Too many assaults. Too much shooting. Too
much death. They had become Wild West desperadoes. He opened his eyes and giggled at the
thought. Maybe they should get decked out in
cowboy garb like Butch Cassidy and the Sun-
dance Kid; like Wyatt Earp and Doc Holiday.

Chico's snores wafted across to the front seat.

"He's a stone psycho," said Rowse to Matt,
speaking about their sleeping companion.

"You notice that even though the beer puts him
out, he never pisses. How can a guy drink that
much beer and never piss?" Matt asked.

Rowse shrugged and scratched his heavily
bearded face. "Hell, he don't piss, I don't sleep.
Six of one . . . half a dozen of another," he said.

Matt began to study the terrain. It was flat,
very flat. It was nothing like Oaktown. He had
been thinking about Oaktown a lot lately, particularly about Julie. What an idiotic sister she
was. When he came home from jail she couldn't
look at him—she was so scared. She probably
thought he was going to sneak into her room at
night and molest her. Yeah, probably that, and
more.

Then he thought of his mother and he grew
sad. She loved him. He was sorry he had to leave,
only for her sake. He was sorry, too, he had stolen all that canned food from the house when he
left, but, hell, he had to eat.

Now there was light. In the distance he could
see gently rolling hills and then flat land—roll
and dip and flat; dip and flat and roll. It was

depressing. They zoomed past small patches of stores that seemed to cling to the roadside.

Rowse had told him they could keep going for years because they were fearless and crazy—and cops were really the stupidest bastards on earth. Matt didn't really know how long their roll would last, but he knew he would die at the end of it. Poor Mom, he thought. Julie would also be at the funeral, he realized. Well, that would be fine. She would be full of remorse at how she had treated him. She would realize what an idiot she had been.

Matt closed his eyes tightly for a moment as if blotting out the vision of his own funeral. When he opened them, there were tears at the corners. The car was now going over a crushed gravel road, bouncing the occupants gently. He realized that he had to stop all the morbid fantasizing. It was all wrong. His sister Julie, he really knew, would dance at his funeral, in her heart. She hated him. And he knew that she wasn't the sweet little hard-working girl that everyone thought she was. She could be cruel and vindictive and very sly.

Rowse pulled up in front of a small roadside grocery store. He and Matt walked inside, leaving Chico asleep in the back.

They ordered containers of coffee and some pound cake and a couple of packs of cigarettes and a six-pack for Chico. Then they took the package outside and ate the cake and drank the coffee while leaning against the fender of the Mustang.

"We just keep heading east," said Rowse.

"To the ocean," Matt said, laughing.

"Right to the ocean."

"And then when we get to the ocean we just drive the goddamn Mustang in, steal a boat, and keep going."

"Right. Steal a boat. Keep going."

Matt crumpled up the empty coffee container and flung it as far as he could. It landed only about five feet away. Matt noticed that the ground he was standing on was hard dirt with a light, almost chalk top. It was ugly—red and brown streaks.

Matt Novick was wearing a one-piece set of blue coveralls that he had picked up when they robbed a gas station in Nevada. He'd always wanted to wear a mechanic's outfit, and this one was really snazzy with the name Chuck sewn over one of the front pockets. But it hadn't worn well. He smelled himself. The coveralls seemed to be absorbing sweat. He needed a damn shower or a lake to jump into.

Rowse suddenly said: "How about a bank, kid, how about a goddamn Texas bank with all that oil money just laying there? I mean, how about two hundred thousand dollars so when we get to the ocean we don't have to steal a boat—we can buy a goddamn ocean liner."

Matt thought about it. He pulled on his hair, which was getting long and matted. He looked almost girlish now—almost pretty with his thin-faced agitated pallor. If they did do a bank, if they survived, if they had big money in their hands—he was sure going to figure out a way to send some to his mother.

There was a noise from the back of the car. Chico was up. He stared dumbly at them. Rowse dropped the six-pack into the back seat to keep Chico happy, and then returned to the front fender to continue the conversation.

"That guy in the store says there's a big town five miles off the next fork. Post office. Liquor store. Supermarket. Movie. Feed dealer. Two banks." Rowse ticked off the many splendors of the town.

Matt thought, Why not. He had conquered fear. He was powerful. Nothing could really stop him but a bullet. And, above all, he no longer thought he was sick or evil. After that thing had happened, after he had attacked the girl and they had sent him to jail, and for a long time after, he considered himself some kind of creature. Something out of the slime. He knew what people in Oaktown thought about him—the lunatic who couldn't control himself. They thought he was a sleazy, sick, grubbing pervert. Girls, women, even old ladies wouldn't look at him . . . wouldn't talk to him—they just moved aside or turned or walked quickly away. But now it was all different. He was clean, free, strong, armed, moving. He was ready to be rich—ready to die.

"The guy inside said the town is called Janesville. What a goddamn stupid name for a town. Who the hell was Jane?"

As Rowse was talking he was drumming his fingers on the fender. It was a gentle sound but somehow threatening. It was as if someone was running lightly over the ground in bare but powerful feet; like an Indian with war paint, running through a forest, trailing a victim.

"How do you rob a bank?" Matt suddenly asked.

"With guns."

"I mean, is it like in the movies? You jump over the tellers' cage?"

"We'll have to figure it out."

"Do we all go in?"

"No, leave Chico in the car."

"Just you and me?"

"Right."

"We'll walk in, show the guns, and tell them to put it in a sack."

"Yeah, a sack."

There was something very funny about that. Matt began to laugh: "We don't have a goddamn sack," he said.

Rowse lit a cigarette and leaned against the fender, contemplating the problem.

"Where do we get a sack?"

"Steal one."

"From who?"

Matt started to laugh again. He could envision three desperadoes with guns drawn bursting into a store and getting a sack; then running into the bank and holding them up with the stolen sack. It was just too funny.

The laughter vanished as quickly as it had arrived. Matt stiffened and pressed his body against the car.

On the shoulder of the road, about one hundred yards away, was a cop car.

"I didn't see it before. Where did it come from?" he whispered, motioning with his hand. Rowse turned and stared at the red and white county vehicle.

"Be cool," Rowse said.

"What's he doing?"

"Checking us out," said Rowse. "Running the license number through the computer."

Matt started to move quickly toward the front door of the car.

"Stay," hissed Rowse, "be cool. The car is still clean. Those people are still sleeping in the motel. They don't even know yet their car is gone. No reports yet. We're clean. Be cool. He's a county cop. He doesn't have anything on us from Nevada or anywhere else. Be cool."

Matt stayed where he was. He thrust his clenched hands into the pockets of his coveralls.

"What do we do?" he asked.

To his horror, Rowse waved and smiled enthusiastically at the cop car.

"Wave, man, wave to the bastard," he told Matt, who did his best, lifting one hand in a feeble greeting.

There was no response from the cop car.

"County cop," said Rowse with derision, "but we're clean. No stolen report on the car. The sonofabitch is just watching us now and he's too far away to ID anything but the car. He knows we can't really be bad guys. I mean, if we were bad guys, would we be standing in the open, waving and smiling and eating cake and drinking coffee? I mean, do bad guys do that?"

Police Officer John Ricks signed off on the radio. The computer said the car was clean. He stared at the young men who were waving to him. He couldn't place them. Maybe kids who worked the night shift at the auto parts factory. Maybe some goofballs from Lucan County, just north, going to the liquor store in Janesville. He had thought he had something. They looked funny. They looked like they weren't going anywhere and hadn't come from anywhere.

Ricks checked the time. Only two hours left on the shift. Well, he thought, next time. He started the engine and turned the car around, heading away from them. He made a mental note.

Matt, Rowse, and Chico entered Janesville just as the town was waking. It was bigger than they had expected: one main east-west street and two smaller streets, one north of the main drag and the other south.

They pulled up in front of the post office and looked around.

"I like that one," Rowse said, pointing to a two-story granite building with a sign on its front that said West Texas Federal Savings and Loan Association.

"Yeah," Rowse continued, "I can see it lying there; all that bread. Pretty, stack on stack. And guarded by three little tellers."

Because they were amateurs, they laid their plans very carefully, as if it were a military campaign that only needed precision to guarantee success. They wouldn't move on the bank until about two-thirty in the afternoon. Sometime during the morning Matt would enter the bank with some cash and buy American Express traveler's checks. He would study the layout of the bank. Then they would park the car on one of the smaller streets and wait. Chico would stay in the car with the .38. Matt and Rowse would do the job, carrying the shotgun and the 9mm.

If it was done right, they could get out of the bank fast, out of Janesville fast, and no one would ID the car. It required that Matt and Rowse spring one block to the car after the holdup. After the job they would hide in a gulley they had located five minutes outside of town for twenty-four hours. Simple. Fast. Wild.

They spent the remainder of the morning eating potato chips and drinking chocolate milk. They bought two large pillowcases to function as money sacks.

Matt got the American Express checks as planned with no trouble. The inside of the bank turned out to be exactly the same as the banks in Oaktown. There was a line of tellers' windows, a separate area of desks, and a large space for the customers to write out deposit slips, et cetera.

When he got back with the information, Rowse laid it all out between mouthfuls of potato chips.

"I got the shotgun. I stay outside the cages. Matt goes behind with the sacks. The tellers open up every goddamn drawer. Matt stuffs every goddamn bill in the sacks. Everyone gets down on the floor. I figure five minutes for the whole thing."

It sounded very good. Matt closed his eyes and tried to sleep. Rowse sucked on a green pill. Chico finished a can of beer and was playing with it—trying to balance the empty can on his forehead.

Matt wondered what his mother was doing right then; was she thinking of him? Was she worried about him? He should send her a postcard. Since he had been living out of a car, he had lost all sense of time and space. It would be almost impossible for him to buy a postcard, address it, stamp it, and mail it.

He wondered what his sister was doing—probably rehearsing her shit for that stupid baseball team. Well, in another few hours, he thought with relish, he would make more money in five minutes than she and the San Diego Chicken would make in a whole year.

Finally, he slept, but fitfully. The smell of his coveralls was like a blanket over him.

At two they began to get ready. They were cramped and anxious. They cleaned and loaded their weapons. They made sure their shoelaces were tied. To avoid being noticed they urinated in empty coffee cups and left them at the bottom of the back seat.

Matt smelled the 9mm weapon. He had only fired it three times during their rampage, but he hadn't hit anyone. He loved its odor, its feel. He loved the way it hung in his hand. This thing, this gun, he realized, was the difference. It was beautiful, it was powerful. It made everyone defer, respect, take notice. Possession of it made him superior to everything he hated, and everything that hated him.

Rowse was beginning to drum his fingers on the wheel of the Mustang. The shotgun was between his legs. He flicked on the radio. The station was holding a Hank Williams retrospective and they were playing "Your Cheating Heart," an old country song from the 1950's.

Rowse was talking numbers as his little green pills started to rev him up: "Fifty thousand, a hundred thousand, a quarter of a mill, man, this time it's for all the marbles."

Chico reached across from the back seat and patted both Rowse and Matt on the shoulder. He showed them the .38, gleaming in his hand.

It was two-fifteen. In ten minutes they would leave the car. A sudden plan came to Matt. After the bank job, after he reached the ocean—he would go away for five years and do nothing. But he would make the bank money grow into a million, five million, ten million. He would go to Monte Carlo and win it all because he no longer feared anything. And then he would go back to Oaktown. He would buy his mother a new house. His sister Julie would no longer hate or fear him; she would look up to him, she would ask his advice. He would buy the goddamn baseball team and make Julie manager, if she wanted. He would buy the whole damn city.

"You crazy?" Rowse asked him, interrupting his fantasy.

"Why?"

"You're sitting there, laughing."

"I was thinking of something," Matt explained, and he realized how much he really hated Oaktown and how he would really rather go back there with guns and blow them all away, than go back with money.

Matt and Rowse left the car at 2:22 P.M. The moment they left Chico got into the front, started up the engine, and let it idle, placing the fully loaded .38 on the seat beside him.

Rowse walked first through the revolving door, and then Matt followed him. There were two customers in the bank and an unarmed uniformed guard who seemed to double as the janitor. Two bank officers were at their desks. Two tellers were at their windows.

The moment they reached the center of the bank, Rowse held up the shotgun with both hands over his head and screamed: "We are going to kill anyone who makes a single sound."

The people froze. Rowse's eyes moved from side to side, larger than life.

Matt held the 9mm weapon with one hand and ran behind the teller's window—the door to the section was wide open. His sacks were stuck in his belt.

Rowse yelled to the tellers: "Open every drawer. Open every drawer or I'm going to blow your head off. Open them. Open them all."

His voice was like a jackhammer.

Matt, standing behind the tellers, could feel their fear. They began to open all the drawers, fumbling with their keys at the bottom ones but finally getting them open.

He could see it was the bottom drawers that held the hundreds and the fifties and large banded packs of twenties. He began to stuff the sacks. He was beginning to get scared now. The tellers refused to look at him. They kept their eyes straight ahead. When he bent near them to reach the money he could see tiny blue veins in their pale necks. They reminded him of the girl he had attacked. Her body had been so white, so pale.

"Get it, boy; get it, boy." Rowse now kept up a steady manic beat of encouragement for Matt, egging him on to greater speed, to more cash stuffed in the sacks.

When the two sacks were filled, Matt hoisted them on his shoulder and walked out from behind the teller cages.

Rowse was laughing now, his crazy eyes glinting in the bank gloom. Grasping the shotgun, he danced over to the teller's cage and threatened them with it. "Five minutes. You stay on the floor for five minutes. One of us will be waiting outside. The first one that steps outside before five minutes is up is dead—real dead." He started to chant, "Five minutes, five minutes," and danced over to the bank executives. He threatened everyone.

They backed out of the bank together, strolled to the corner, and then sprinted the one block to the car.

Chico was waiting—grinning. They jumped

into the back seat and the Mustang drove lei-
surely out of Janesville to a small gully five miles
outside of town, just off the main highway.

Once parked, they said nothing for a long time.
The sweetness, the exhaustion, the daring of it
all rendered them speechless.

Then they counted the money. Exactly
$309,660 in tens, twenties, fifties, and hundreds.
They were rich. They were the salt of the earth.
They sat, rich, in the Mustang, surrounded by
barren rocks and sliding mounds of dirt. They
could wait it out. Their time was soon.

John Ricks checked the old alarm clock chained
to the front mirror of his pickup truck by lighting
a match. The hands read 10:20. Since he was due
on duty at midnight, that meant he had to kill
over an hour because he could make the drive to
the barracks in twenty minutes.

He had started out an hour earlier than usual
because he couldn't sleep; and he couldn't sleep
because he was furious at himself; and he was
furious at himself because he had heard about
the bank job on the radio, and the two gunmen
identified were the same who had been standing
beside the Mustang—the one he had checked out
on the computer.

He had felt then that they were wrong, bad,
funny. He should have gone further.

The only odd thing about the radio report was
that it said the robbers had escaped without anyone having identified the vehicle used.

He pulled off the road at Junior's for a beer. It

was not something he did often—it was very bad policy to drink anything before going on duty—but it wasn't often he had to kill so much time. Ricks had two beers in Junior's and left at eleven-thirty.

Halfway to the barracks he pulled off the road by a stunted sycamore tree. He walked to the tree and urinated against the trunk.

As he turned to start back toward his pickup truck, his eyes caught something off in the distance.

He stopped and waited. It was a light—a match—someone was lighting a cigarette in the gulley below. It was a very odd place for someone to go to have a smoke.

He moved quickly and quietly to the edge of the gulley. A car was parked there.

Even in the dim moonlight he could see that it was the yellow Mustang.

He ran back to the pickup and removed his small snub-nosed .38 from the glove compartment and a .30-.30 deer rifle from behind the front seat. He should call in, he realized; he should get some backup. But he didn't. This one he decided to do himself—to take both of them alone.

Ricks checked the weapons and slipped their safeties off. He dug out of the toolbox a megaphone, a large flashlight, and some handcuffs.

He felt oddly light-headed, happy. This was going to be the biggest bust a county cop had made in five years.

He moved carefully, picking his way through

the darkness until the car was about fifty feet away from him down the gulley incline. He no longer saw the telltale cigarette light.

The large flashlight went on.

"This is the police. You are surrounded and under arrest. Come out of the vehicle with your hands over your head. You will not be harmed. Leave all your weapons exactly where they are. Come out of the vehicle with your hands over your head."

The megaphone projected the voice like a cannon.

There was no response.

Ricks moved closer, propping the flashlight against a rock so that the light remained steady against the car door.

Nothing was moving. No one was coming out.

John Ricks wasn't going to play with these jokers.

He gently rested the rifle against his leg, and, holding the small .38 revolver in a combat crouch, fired three bullets through the front windshield.

Rowse came out shooting and running, the shotgun blast peppering Ricks's legs. He fell down, firing as he went, his second shot hitting Rowse in the eye, killing the biker instantly.

He caught sight of the other one, rolling out the side door. Ricks picked up the rifle and began firing.

Matt, having reached safety beneath the car, aimed carefully. It was so easy. Seven 9mm slugs were stitched across Ricks's chest.

Then all was quite. Matt rose slowly. He saw no other cops.

"There was only one, Chico, only one," he said.

Matt walked to the dead cop and kicked him twice. He grinned. He kicked him a third time. He looked up and saw Chico standing next to him. Matt bent down to collect the cop's handgun.

The tire iron hit Matt Novick just at the base of the neck. He fell heavily, his spinal cord severed.

Chico picked up Ricks's gun and rammed it into Matt's mouth, pulling the trigger twice. Then he went back to the car, hoisted the two pillowcases filled with cash over his shoulder, and walked out of the gulley.

Texas State Troopers Anslagen and Rivera found the yellow Mustang and the three bodies five hours later.

Rivera opened the trunk during an exhaustive search of the vehicle.

He found something that resembled a wolf skin; only the teeth and claws were obviously made of scrap metal.

Wrapped inside the skin were thirty-one cans of Campbell's soup—primarily chicken noodle and tomato.

27

THEY huddled around the obscenity. The plucked-out eyes seemed to embody all the horror . . . all the filth . . . all the stupidity the world was capable of.

No one knew what to do with Roger Randle's eyes, lying like poached eggs on the small memorial stone of the long-dead Indian girl.

"Where're Bunny and Tim Shea?" Tournier asked.

"I saw them up by the flatbed truck," Lambert answered.

Dominic stood up. Next to him was Roth, who had helped him up and was now grasping one of Dominic's arms as if it were possible for him to fall again.

"We have to go in there," Tournier said, pointing into the dump. "They're in there . . . the killer—and what's left of Roger. We have to end it now!"

He stared at the others and then repeated: "We have to end it now."

There was no reply. Lambert was waving up the slope at the musicians, who didn't know what to do, having been interrupted in the middle of the ceremony.

"Keep them the hell away from here," Tournier said to Lambert, and the detective cupped his hands and yelled those instructions to them.

Roth, one hand supporting Dominic and the other nervously smoothing one leg of his pants, found himself silently reciting all parts of the human eye under his breath, trying to maintain a clinical attitude to what he had seen.

"I told you this was crazy," Dominic whispered in Roth's ear. "I told you it was something else."

Roth didn't understand what Dominic was saying. Tournier, he felt, had been right. The killer had been flushed—at a terrible cost.

Dominic shook from Roth's grip and hobbled over to Tournier. He grabbed the police chief and held on tightly: "What if Roger is still alive? What if he's been dragged deep into the dump? What if his eyes were ripped out but he's still alive? What if he knows what has happened? What if he's being pulled apart somewhere in there? What if he can feel the horror? Taste it? Smell it? But can't see it?"

Tournier pushed the old man off, with distaste. "Get a hold of yourself," he spat at him, and Dominic did, suddenly ashamed of his outburst.

"Come here," Tournier said to the others, and knelt down on the ground, picking up a small stick.

They gathered round him. All of them kept their faces averted from the mutilated eyes, which were beginning to dribble down the stone, which were beginning to lose shape and consistency and substance in the damp night air.

"There are three old access roads in this dump. Two toward the outer edges and one in the center. Once one gets deep into the dump there are connecting roads to each."

Lambert shook his head: "I see no roads."

Tournier responded: "They're all overgrown. They aren't roads any longer, they're barely discernible paths."

Lambert nodded. Tournier sketched the three routes onto the ground.

"Roth and Dominic take this one to the north. Lambert, you take the south one. I'll go to the center route. Take some long sticks with you to beat a path and keep the shrubs out of your face."

He pulled out his weapon and checked it: a .25 caliber Beretta.

"Do you have that ankle piece?" he asked Lambert, who took a small pistol from his ankle holster in response. In the other hand Lambert held a particularly ugly-looking semiautomatic carbine with a folding stock.

"Give it to Roth," Tournier told his associate, who then handed it to the physician, and silently, in pantomime, detailed how simple it was to work.

"When one of us—any of us—finds anything, sees anything, call out. If an emergency, fire three shots. Is that clear?" Tournier waited for an affirming nod from each of them before continuing.

"Do you know what I am going to do now?" he asked. His voice had become high-pitched and tremulous.

No one answered. Tournier turned quickly and with his arm violently swept the organs off the stone and into the dirt. He stamped on them like a deranged child.

"We are going to end this whole mess now, tonight, forever. Do you understand?"

"It dances," Dominic whispered. "I heard it dance. It was coming to get me, just as it got Roger and the others."

Roth nodded but did not respond to Dominic's words. He picked up an old rod of rusted steel from the sodden ground. It could be used to break open the path.

"Let's go," Tournier said, regaining his composure, and they all walked into the overgrown dump, each on his own path—Dominic and Roth together.

The first hundred yards for Tournier was easy. There was little overhead growth, so he just trod the bushes down. Then it became difficult, and he no longer heard either Lambert or Roth and Dominic on their respective paths.

He held his flashlight in one hand, a stick in the other, and the Beretta was in his belt.

Tournier was happy to be working alone. It

had been fifteen years since he was actively in
the field as a working cop. He was a good administrator, but he had always been best doing
investigative work. He was smart, brave, inquis-
itive, yet lacking arrogance. That was why he
had moved up—that was why he was chief.

There was another reason why he was' glad he
was alone. He now understood that what they
were facing was not human in any traditional
sense. Roger had been mutilated too swiftly, with
too much stealth and power. No man could have
done it. No three men could have done it. And
he did not trust the others; they were too frightened of the reality they faced. They were too
young. They had not seen enough. Even Dominic, who was much older than he, was a baseball
player, a child in an old man's body.

He walked deeper into the dump. He felt oddly
elated, and he was a bit ashamed of that elation.
His plan had indeed worked, but it had cost
Roger his life. The mock ceremony for the Indian
girl, Highsmith, had moved him. As he was
speaking the words, he had truly thought about
her—the memory buried in garbage for twenty-
five years. He understood the beast—whoever
and whatever it was; the death of a child could
not go unavenged.

It was becoming harder to move. Generations
of garbage seemed to emerge from the ground.
Plastic, wood, metal, rotted unmentionables. It
was as if he were fighting his way through a perverse garden of Eden.

The colors he could make out in the night were

muted—dull greens, browns, blacks. The flashlight revealed strange forms, strange juxtaposi-
tions of nature and society, like a small ugly tree
wrapped around the decaying rusted remnants of
a child's tricycle. Which was feeding on which?
Which was forcing which to bend?

He went deeper into the dump, moving more
quickly, beating out a path as if he were an ex-
plorer in an Amazonian jungle.

Every five or ten minutes he stopped and listened. There were no calls or shouts from the
others. He lost track of time, and although his
enthusiasm for the chase did not flag, he knew
he was slowing down.

How far inside the dump was he? He didn't
know. When would the others reach a converg-
ing path? He didn't know.

He wished his grandmother could somehow
perceive what he was doing. She, above all, understood the irrational world. She believed that
it could break in and destroy all that had been
so laboriously built . . . that it could create the
horrors we deserve.

He paused, realizing that he had reached some
high ground, a sort of plateau. Was this the spine
of the dump?

As he stood there, resting, thinking, an odor
wafted over the space. At first it was gentle, just
a strangeness, yet totally different from the almost fermented odor of the dump.

But as he stood there it began to build, to
gather strength, to permeate the air.

It became fetid, almost choking. He could not

identify the odor except that he felt—he felt very strongly—that it came from something alive.

He became alert. The odor seemed to infiltrate his body.

It became oppressive. He started to move off the plateau, toward the shrubs again.

An object hurtled out of the brush and toward him . . . so suddenly and with such force that he could not evade it.

It struck against his chest, causing him to gasp for air.

The object fell to the ground. He shone the flashlight on it.

Roger Randle's eyeless, severed head lay like a grotesque eggplant in front of him.

He stared down, uncomprehending, at the shriveled sphere.

From the perimeter of the space, in the brush, he heard a sound. A rustling. Something was moving. It was moving steadily, rhythmically.

Tournier remembered what Dominic had claimed about his experience by the abandoned freight cars: that the thing had danced.

It was there in the bushes. His time had come. Good, he thought, good.

Was the dance a celebration of his forthcoming death?

He dropped the stick and the flashlight next to the severed head.

He closed his eyes, trying to locate by sound alone the creature that was dancing in the bushes.

It was as if he had waited all his life to find the terror . . . to embrace it . . . to meet it.

The Beretta was like an extra finger, part of him.

He waited. He listened. He opened his eyes— they were acclimated to the darkness.

The dance stopped. There was silence and that smell.

He could sense where it was—in the bushes. In a large clump of saw grass. Off to his right.

He crouched and gathered his strength. It was beginning to grow—a shadow. It seemed to be spreading over the ground, to be filling all the bushes with life and death.

From where he crouched he could make out the outline of Roger's head. That poor soul, he thought, that poor innocent soul. And there welled up in him a violent, passionate hatred for that murderous thing . . . for all the horrors it had caused.

Tournier leaped into the bushes.

It was on him in a second.

Its grip was so sudden and so powerful that the breath seemed to be jerked out of his body in spasms. His head reeled.

Tournier held the Beretta. He did not drop it. He waited until his face had brushed against something alive.

He gagged. He tasted something noxious and alive.

He emptied the Beretta into his attacker, yelling out half-choked screams as he heard the bullets strike.

The grip around him relaxed for just a moment after the bullets smacked home, and then intensified again. His mouth was filling with blood. Was his throat gone?

Tournier thought: I have to open my eyes and see it. I have to see his face before I die.

He struggled for clarity. He fought to open his eyes and look.

He saw it. He relaxed and smiled. He thought of his grandmother. And then a horrible pain ripped through his stomach and up into his chest. He screamed.

Dominic and Roth heard the shots and the scream from the northern section of the dump. They didn't know who it was.

Lambert heard it from the southern sector and knew instantly who it was—Tournier.

They abandoned their assigned paths and began to crash through the bushes, stumbling, cursing, beating about them with their sticks. They stopped from time to time to listen carefully, but there were no other sounds.

Then Dominic and Roth heard Lambert call out. They answered him. The three men met on a swampy piece of ground.

"Up there," Lambert said, pointing. "The scream came from up there, from the high ground."

They pushed on, exhausted, desperate, the sweat dripping from their faces.

"Look," Lambert whispered.

Hanging, impaled on a small tree, was the headless corpse of Roger.

They started to run.

They saw Tim Shea next. His genitals were stuffed into his open mouth. His hands held his entire viscera. He was a gutted corpse.

Tournier was twenty feet from him. His heart had been ripped from his body and lay in the dirt. His throat had been sliced from ear to ear. The Beretta was still clutched in his hand.

Lambert knelt down. Dominic wavered, trying to catch his breath. His eyes were blinded by tears.

Roth shone his flashlight past Tournier.

"There," he cried out, as the light revealed another corpse.

But it was unlike any corpse they had ever seen.

They approached slowly, silently. Now all three flashlights were focused on the unidentified corpse.

It had once been a human body. But the skeleton structure of the body was totally extruded from the skin.

And while the flesh and contorted features of the corpse were that of a woman . . . the skeletal structure that imprisoned the body was that of a large wolf.

It was as if a wolf skeleton had been burned onto the flesh, blood, and sinew of a human body and had taken root there—had grown there.

Then Dominic saw the long golden hair flowing out of the bullet-smashed head.

He knew he was looking at the crushed and

contorted remnant of Bunny Bunsen's beautiful
face.

He crossed himself.

A terrible odor came from the corpse.

Roth, with as much medical curiosity as re-
vulsion, knelt beside the corpse and ran his hand
lightly along the ridges of the extruded wolf skeleton. In his medical training he had heard of ba-
bies born with skeletons on the outside of their
bodies. But this was literally a massive lupine su-
perstructure that seemed to have become an or-
ganic part of her body . . . that seemed to have
broken through from inside her, as if it had
grown beneath the skin, transforming the human
structure.

"No," Dominic suddenly screamed and, lung-
ing forward, pushed Roth away from the corpse.
It was just in time.

A second later, a crazed Lambert emptied his
carbine into the strange, now harmless corpse.
Bullet after bullet—forty-two rounds—splintered, tore, ravaged the heap.

And then Lambert staggered, dropping the
carbine, and fell.

Roth ignored what had happened. He moved
back to the smoldering heap.

"Dominic," he asked, in a gentle, pedantic
voice, "do you see what happened to her? Do you
understand? It has nothing to do with werewolf
legends. She did not turn into a wolf. A skeleton
broke through her flesh and encased her in a
wolf's musculature. Then it receded. Then it
broke through. It was a skeletal transformation."

The wonder of it all dazed Roth. He stared at the heap and knew he was speaking nonsense.

"But why and how?" he suddenly added.

"And why did she kill?" he continued, after a reflective pause.

"And why did she mutilate?" He paused again. Then he yelled at Dominic: "Who did it to her?"

Lowering his voice, getting control of himself, he asked: "And, oh my God, Dominic, was she conscious when it was happening to her?"

Roth reached a hand through the bloody extruded skeleton to the remains of the once beautiful face. He stroked it.

Dominic was weeping now, his eyes fixed on the yellow strands of hair.

Roth asked: "How did a human skeleton, Bunny Bunsen's skeleton, transform itself within the body into that of a rabid wolf? How did it then erupt outside of the skin, encasing her in murder?"

Roth stared at Dominic, as if the old man, in his grief, could provide answers.

Then Roth walked over to Lambert. The detective seemed to be hyperventilating slightly, but he would be fine. Then he walked to Tournier's corpse. What willful vengeance! He had never seen such carnage in the States, and only once before in his life, when he had been in Nigeria and a train had derailed. Twenty had been crushed to death and hundreds were hurt. But that was understandable; that was malfunctioning technology.

He stared around at the enveloping fog. How

did he get here? Why had he been forced or lured or cajoled into seeing what he had seen? No one would believe it. No one could be told. It was so bizarre, and the sadness of it all was that it meant absolutely nothing. Roth did not believe in the transcendental. He believed only in what there was—short and brutish lives, governed by chance, alleviated only a bit by love or music or laughter.

It would take a great deal of Mozart over many years to wash out the memory of that lovely young woman, encased in a beast's skeleton, wreaking her bloody vengeance on innocents. He shook his head as if to clear out the confusion. Another question came to him. Who is innocent? He had the odd feeling that he could never again touch another mask of the Coastal Indians. For if the shaman had indeed used Bunny Bunsen to call the wolf spirits home—then a power existed both in their masks and their minds that nauseated him . . . that made them beyond the pale of humanity. He grimaced. He was thinking like a fool. No Indian shaman could graft a killer wolf's musculature onto a live human body.

Suddenly, standing there amid the dead, the mutilated, the grieving, the unexplained—he longed to be back in his ward, among the alcoholics, where he could help.

28

THE headline in the paper the next day was bold and black. One word took up the entire page: TRAGEDY.

The story went on to describe something that never happened. The newspaper reported that a flatbed truck carrying two searchlights fell down a slope at the old city dump—crushing to death Chief of Police Tournier, Bunny Bensen, Roger Randle, and Tim Shea.

The truck then exploded and burned the victims until they became unrecognizable.

The newspaper briefly described the memorial service that was scheduled for that same day. And then printed capsule biographies of each of the victims.

Dominic stared at the paper without reading it. At eleven in the morning Victor's was empty except for himself and the bartender who was getting ready for the lunch-hour traffic.

It was Lambert who had constructed the cov-

erup and carried it out quickly and perfectly—
gathering the corpses together into a pile, running the truck off the road onto them, and then
torching the truck and the bodies. Dominic and
Roth had agreed to it. What else could they do?
What would have been gained in this case from
broadcasting the truth? What was the truth?

Dominic sipped the large glass of water in front
of him; then sipped a cold cup of coffee; then
sipped the brandy. Usually, he would never drink
in the morning.

He had not slept since those horrid and bizarre
events took place. Roth had driven him home, it
was morning by then, and he had sat in his house
for about fifteen minutes before realizing that
sleep was totally impossible. So he went for a
long walk, only to end up at Victor's.

He knew now why he alone had been spared.
He knew now that the beast indeed had been
lying in wait for him at the abandoned freight
cars; that the beast, whose heart and soul was
Bunny's, but whose body was that of a twisted
killer, could not kill him—because Bunny loved
him, and no matter how she had been bewitched
or possessed or transformed, she could not mutilate the Coach.

She must have loved him a great deal, Dominic thought, and began to cry as he remembered
her bullet-ridden body—her golden hair made
obscene by the skeletal ridges that had erupted
through her skin and tormented her body into a
beast of prey.

Then he braced himself, sat back, and had an-

other sip of brandy, noticing that his hand shook
a bit.

A man started bringing in kegs of beer through
the front door. Dominic watched him, confused.
He couldn't believe that the world was proceed-
ing as if nothing had happened. But it was. The
city, the state, the nation, the world, was simply
going about its business. They didn't know what
really happened in the Oaktown dump, and if
they knew, they wouldn't believe it.

Roth had said to him on the drive home:
"When there are too many questions to answer
about a problem—just leave it alone."

Dominic didn't have too many questions. He
had only a few. Who had captured Bunny? What
had enslaved her? Who had turned her into a
monster? Who had destroyed her?

The brandy was beginning to get to him. He
was going to miss her dreadfully. He was going
to suffer every day knowing what she had en-
dured, and forced others to endure.

He pushed back the glasses on the table and
leaned his head down on the wood. Every time
he tried to visualize her face, he could only think
of her encased in that skeletal beast; half woman,
half animal, the yellow hair streaked with her
own blood as well as her victims'.

Then he thought of her photo, in the collage,
the one she had given him years ago. She had
given it to him as a birthday present. She had cut
out several pictures of herself that had been taken
when she was living in France and placed them
on a large sheet of matting. They were beautiful

pictures; her hair was long and golden and she was wearing sundresses and no shoes. She had obtained old pictures of Dominic in his playing days with the San Francisco Seals and placed them in the collage, including a wonderful shot of Dominic and Joe DiMaggio chatting together at the batter's cage, just before the Yankee Clipper went up to the majors.

Remembering the photo collage made him recall that it was no longer in his possession. He had returned it to Bunny about six months ago for her to give to a friend of hers who could fix the matting—which had torn and cracked. God, he thought, now I'll never get it back.

He sat straight up and finished the brandy. That wouldn't do at all. Those photos had somehow caught their special relationship while she was alive, and now, more than ever, he must have them.

Bunny had once told him: "The house is yours. Anytime. Just make yourself at home. You know where I hide the key. Watch television there, sleep there, do anything you want. You don't have to clear it with me. Anyway, you know that I'm rarely home. My house is yours, Dominic, understand?"

He got to his feet and left Victor's. It was a twenty-minute walk to Bunny's house. He paused for a moment at the large tree and then turned into the driveway. The key was where it was always hidden: in the mouth of an ornamental dolphin that was perched right next to the garage doors. He let himself in the back door and walked through the kitchen without turning on the light. He remembered last placing the collage to be repaired in an unused bedroom on the second floor.

He was halfway up the stairs when he realized someone else was in the house; someone else was upstairs.

He stopped. The thief was going through the drawers in Bunny's bedroom—he could hear him pulling them out and overturning them.

Dominic didn't know what to do. No lights were on and the midmorning sun had only partially penetrated the shuttered gloom.

He could see a long-necked vase on a small table at the top of the stairs. He walked softly up the remaining steps and grasped it with two hands; it was heavy, a good weapon.

The thief was ripping Bunny's room apart. The door was wide open.

Dominic was frightened and exhausted. After the previous night he really couldn't handle much more activity.

He tiptoed across the threshold and saw the thief bent over. Fury welled up in him at the sight of this human scavenger, robbing a house less than twenty-four hours after the owner had died.

He took one step into the room and screamed: "Stop."

The thief froze for a moment, absolutely still, and then bolted for the window near the bed.

Dominic caught him with the vase before he reached the window—bringing the object down hard on the intruder's back and neck. There was a sickening thud and the thief was sent sprawling.

Breathing heavily, his hands trembling, Dominic went to the side wall and flicked the light on.

He could not believe what he saw.

Jackie Cannon lay on the floor moaning.

He was wearing a filthy overcoat, under which were the hospital pajamas. He was white as a sheet.

"What the hell are you doing here?" Dominic demanded.

Cannon just shook his head.

"How'd you get out of the hospital?"

"I walked out," he muttered, and propped himself up against the side of the bed.

Dominic was confused. He stared at the weakened, pathetic alcoholic.

"I walked out when I learned what happened last night."

"How the hell did you find out what happened?" Dominic asked.

"Oh, Dominic, I know, I know." And his response was so sad, so wise, so filled with awareness of the real tragedy rather than the version described in the newspapers—that Dominic immediately understood that Cannon was not there as a common thief.

"What are you here after, Jackie?"

"I can't tell you, Dominic, I can't."

Dominic knelt beside the man, showing him the vase: "Many people died horribly last night, Jackie. And before that, children were murdered

and mutilated. Bunny is dead. I have nothing
left. I am going to hurt you very badly, Jackie,
if you don't tell me the truth."

Cannon shook his head wearily.

Dominic felt the anger, the hatred, like a large
ball in his chest.

He savagely swung the vase. It smashed against
Jackie Cannon's eyes—splitting the lid and sending a geyser of blood spurting out.

Jackie whimpered.

"Do you want to die, Jackie? Do you want to
die?" Dominic asked, showing him the vase
again.

Jackie shook his head.

The cabinet, Dominic suddenly thought, the
cabinet. Bunny kept brandy there. He walked to
the cabinet and flung the door open. A half bottle of Martell stared at him.

He pulled the cork and let Jackie smell it. An
ugly scene, he realized, but the whole world was
ugly now.

"It's yours, Jackie, if you tell me."

Cannon stared at Dominic and then at the bottle. He seemed to be lost in thought. Finally, he
nodded and Dominic gave him the bottle. He
took a long drink, coughed, gagged, and then
clumsily lit a cigarette.

"I was looking for the shells," he said.

"What shells?"

Jackie reached into his pocket and brought out
the shells he always carried.

"Do you remember that night in the bar?" he
asked Dominic. "When you found me in the la-

dies' room with Bunny? When she thought I was a crazed rapist?"

"Yes."

"I was there to place shells like these in her pocket without her knowing."

"Did you?"

"Yes."

"Why?"

"They were shells that carried the wolf spirits of my people. They were blessed by the shaman. They would bring her under the spell of the wolf spirits. They would turn her into an instrument of terror."

"But why, Jackie? Why?"

"Help me onto the bed."

Dominic helped him up, placed him on the bed, propped up against the pillows, holding the cigarette in one hand and the brandy bottle in the other. Dominic took out his handkerchief, wet it in the small adjoining bathroom, and staunched Jackie's bleeding eye.

"It's a long story, Dominic."

"Tell it to me. Tell me how we won death."

"It concerns my people."

"You mean the Indians?"

"Yes. What do you know about my people?"

"Only what Roth told us. About the wolf spirits and your rituals."

Jackie Cannon took a long drink.

"I will tell you what you can comprehend. I will tell you why it happened."

He took another long swig, then lit a fresh cigarette, and began his narrative.

Dominic listened and said nothing as it unfolded, absorbing the astonishing tale.

"The Indian girl fell into the swamp in 1963. Her father was a shaman. His English name is John True. He begged the city to recover the body. They would not. That meant her spirits would forever be with the wolves. She would never be ransomed. She would never rest in peace. John True went to Walter Bunsen, who owned many earth-moving machines. He proposed a bargain to him. He told Walter Bunsen that he would guarantee that the Oaktown Wolves won the championship of the Pacific Coast League that season, even though they were in last place—if Walter Bunsen recovered the body. Walter asked how John True could do that. John True told him he could make very big magic. At first Walter laughed. Then he grew curious. Then he realized he had nothing to lose. He told John True he would make a bargain. If the Wolves won the 1963 PCL championship, he would dig up the whole goddamn swamp to find the child. They shook hands and drank on the bargain. John True gave Walter some blood. He told Walter that at least three players must paint the back of their necks. He, John True, would do the rest. He would make big magic. John True did make good magic. The Wolves won the 1963 championship. He went to Walter to collect. Walter threw him out of the office, saying the whole thing was a goddamn joke. Walter refused to dig up the swamp. John True became morose. He started to drink very heavily. He was stopped

by a cop while driving his car drunk. The cop
insulted him. John True beat the cop to death.
He was sentenced to life imprisonment. He served
twenty-five years and was paroled in February.
John True came to see me. He told me to place
the shells on Walter Bunsen's daughter. John
True told me that he would avenge his daughter's spirits. John True told me he was making
big magic again. He would fasten the wolf onto
the body of Walter Bunsen's daughter. She would
destroy the world that had betrayed the People.
Only then, John True said, would the wolf spirits
be avenged and release his daughter's spirit to
come home. John True told me he performed the
Wolf Dance each night in his cell for twenty-five
years. He told me his magic is very powerful. He
told me he would kill me if I did not obey. John
True came to the hospital last night. He told me
what had happened. He was there, hiding in the
swamp. He had a vision there. The wolf spirits
had been satiated. His daughter's spirit had been
released. He will make no more magic, he told
me. He ordered me to find the shells that I had
placed on Bunny and bury them in Bunsen Stadium."

When the narrative was finished, Dominic
went into the small bathroom and found a glass.
He poured himself some brandy from Jackie's
rapidly emptying bottle.

He didn't know how to respond to what Jackie
had told him. It was like hearing a fairy tale that
somehow had come true. There was nothing to
say. The individual elements were so bizarre, but

the central theme of the pact—the idea that
Walter Bunsen would make a bargain with the
devil to win—rang true. Walter would do anything to win. And the devil in this case was an
Indian medicine man who had lost a daughter.
What the Indian medicine man didn't know, for
all his magic, was that Walter Bunsen never paid
off, never kept his word—the man had been a
liar.

He felt no hatred, oddly, for John True, re-
gardless of the horrors he had set into motion.
Rather he felt a sense of awe for a man who could
spend twenty-five years in the penitentiary waiting for his chance, building up the power of his
magic, dancing for thousands of nights, waiting,
always waiting. If he, Dominic, was a father,
and believed that his daughter's spirit was
doomed to be forever unredeemed, he, too,
would use whatever power he could. But never
murder and mutilation. Never wholesale slaughter. John True was mad, he thought. They were
all mad—the Indians, Walter Bunsen, all of
them. Dominic stared at Jackie, who was now
calm but exhausted after his short narrative.
Dominic marveled at how little he knew about
the man. It was that way with the Indians. If
Patricia Highsmith was John True's daughter,
why didn't they have the same names? Had she
been his adoptive daughter or his natural daughter? And what did it matter? Had Jackie told him
everything or was he being sly? It was so strange;
the whole thing from beginning to end was so
strange.

He turned on Jackie suddenly, violently: "Look how many were destroyed. Look at the horror that was visited on Bunny. Did you see her, Jackie? Her body was violated. Her body was twisted into that of a crazed wolf. Her flesh, her face—it was made horrible. Look at what she was forced to do. Look at the way she killed those children."

And then the anger drained out of Dominic. He reached over and laid his hand on Jackie Cannon's arm in a comradely fashion, saying, "Bunny had a box in the other room. She kept odds and ends there."

"I can't get up," Jackie said.

Dominic walked into the other bedroom, found the box, opened it, and saw the shells on a string. He found the photo collage also, behind the door. It had never been fixed. He walked back and dropped the shells into Jackie's hand.

"Will you bury them for me?" Jackie asked.

"Where did you say?"

"In the stadium."

"Why not?" Dominic said, and took the shells back. He'd bury them. He'd bury the whole god-damn thing. There was no understanding . . . no resolution . . . no revenge. Just get rid of the whole long, ugly, insane nightmare. Yes, he'd bury the goddamn shells so deep . . .

Jackie's eye had begun to bleed again from the blow of the vase. Dominic reached out to staunch it again with his handkerchief. As they sat close together, tied to each other by blood and base-ball and the knowledge of what had occurred—

Jackie whispered something into Dominic's ear, as a child whispers to a father.

"I can't hear you," Dominic said.

"I said," Jackie repeated, this time out loud, "that if I was brave none of this would have happened. If I was brave I would not have placed those shells on Bunny."

"Who is brave?" Dominic asked sardonically, of no one if particular.

What happened next happened very quickly. Jackie Cannon shoved the brandy bottle into Dominic's chest, leaped up, ran to the closed window, and flung himself through.

His body splintered the glass and the entire frame. No one would ever know if he thought he was leaping to freedom or death. No one would ever know if he was trying to escape from the room or from his life. He died instantly, of a broken neck.

29

THE enormous tragedy of the spring had, in a sense, broken the heart of the team and the city.

Dominic, after much persuasion, had agreed to come out of retirement and manage the team until the end of the season. It was, he realized, the least he could do for Bunny. He took over the job on June 1.

By September 1, the Oaktown Wolves were in last place, sixteen and a half games behind league-leading Vancouver. Attendance had grown sparse. The wolf mascot and the ball girls had been gently fired.

On September 4, at the end of the first game of a three-game series with Phoenix, which Oaktown lost 9–1, Dominic was being interviewed by the regular sports columnist of the *Oaktown Logger*.

They sat in the seldom-used offices of the club, beneath the stadium. Dominic had showered and changed into his street clothes. His hair was still wet.

The reporter, whose name was Triandos, got right to the point: "Coach, attendance is way down. We're in the basement. People still can't seem to get over all that death. Let's face it. Are we finally seeing the end of the Oaktown Wolves? Are we finally seeing the end of the last independent team in the PCL?"

"I don't know what you mean."

"I mean, are the rumors true? Is the franchise over? Are the Wolves being sold? And relocated?"

"I'm the field manager. That's all. I'm not the general manager. The actual financial operation of the team is now being handled by the bank and a committee that was established after Bunny died."

"I know you're only the manager. But surely you have some inside information."

"They tell me nothing. I'm an interim manager."

"Okay. I'm not going to press that," said Triandos, as if he were being very generous, "but what I really want to know, and I think our readers want to know, is how do you account for the Wolves' collapse this season."

"I can't."

"I mean—what happened?"

Dominic swung around on the swivel chair, and then swung around again.

"The season isn't over yet," he cautioned.

"Shit. Do you think this is going to be another

1963 miracle year? Suddenly you're going to turn it around? Here you are, September fourth, sixteen and a half games back."

Dominic didn't answer. Triandos took a different tack and pushed on.

"I think what the fans really don't understand is the hitting collapse."

"A lot of guys had a bad year at the same time. It happens," Dominic said.

"We're not talking about a bad year. We're talking about a catastrophe. Your third, fourth, and fifth batters in the lineup have a combined average of .231. I mean, Dominic, with that kind of hitting you couldn't win a Little League division."

Dominic was never interested in averages and statistics. He just wanted to get out of there, to end the interview—so he nodded gravely, affirming the reporter's statistical brilliance. But Triandos rambled on, interviewing himself basically. Dominic listened and nodded.

Finally Triandos slapped his notebook shut and started to rise; he caught himself halfway, stopped, and said to Dominic: "The team misses her. The city misses her."

Dominic nodded.

"It's funny," said Triandos, "how in such a short space of time she brought some class to the Oaktown Wolves. She loved baseball. She was something special."

And then Triandos was gone. Dominic sat, as he now often sat, not knowing what to do. His friends were all dead.

He could call Roth to meet him at Victor's—they had become friendly—but it was probably too late for the physician.

He wasn't sorry he had agreed to manage the team until the end of the season, and it really didn't bother him that much that they were in the cellar. He had been there before.

What really bothered him was that he hadn't been able to get close to the players. He had thought his presence would pull them together in the face of the tragedy—he thought that pulling them together would translate into baseball terms.

But he had been wrong. His managing was totally out of synch. He couldn't get the team to mesh . . . to play . . . and they began to crumble. They began to leave men on base. They began to make crucial errors. They stopped hustling. They started missing signals. It was like a blanket, inexorably being drawn over their heads, suffocating their game.

The phone in the office jangled. Dominic let it ring. When it stopped ringing he walked out of the dugout and into the stadium and then out the right-field exit, which was closer to Victor's.

He passed the small patch of sod near the fence where he had buried the shells as Jackie Cannon had requested.

At Victor's he took his usual booth, sliding in, acutely aware that never again would he see Roger and Bunny slide in across from him, eager to do a postmortem on the game.

No, never again. The bartender brought him

a beer and a brandy. He was too old not to drink heavily anymore.

People stopped by briefly to greet him; to make small baseball chatter; to give suggestions as to who to play and who to bench.

Many stopped by just to give a few words of encouragement . . . to tell him there was plenty of time left to turn it around . . . to make the season a success.

Dominic smiled and nodded in agreement with whatever was said to him, without offering any encouragement for further chatter.

Then the visitors vanished and left him in peace. He settled down for a long siege in the booth . . . drinking as slowly as he could . . . trying to dispel the memories . . . trying to retrieve the memories . . . trying to flee from the dreaded but true notion that he was an old fool, totally and irrevocably alone . . . trying to avoid the realization that what he had loved to excess all his life—baseball—might just as well be meaningless.

He dozed intermittently in the soft light and sounds of the bar.

At one point he fell into a deep, troubled nap and dreamed about poor Larrabee.

When he awoke with a start, his mouth very dry and sour, he found himself staring at the wall clock across the bar. It read forty-one minutes past midnight.

Then he brought his eyes from the clock, and to his astonishment he saw a figure standing, silently, without movement, about five feet away from the booth.

The figure, a man, was very, very tall. He was wearing workmen's clothes. His hands hung down by his sides. Suddenly, without any exchange of words, he knew he was staring at the Indian shaman John True.

Dominic knew it as well as he knew his own name. And the moment he knew it, he waited for the rage to grow in him; he waited for the hatred to boil up for this fiend in front of him— this man who had somehow harnessed the ugliest forces of that other world and brought them to earth to destroy and mutilate and kill. But neither rage nor hatred came.

Then the stranger took one long stride and slid into the booth opposite him.

Dominic pushed what was left of the brandy toward him, and he emptied the glass with a toss.

John True lit a cigarette. Up close, his swarthy face was lined like a railroad track.

Dominic watched him smoke. He felt relaxed with John True across from him, very relaxed. As he stared at the Indian he began to feel a sense of elation; a sense of triumph. It grew in his chest. It felt good.

He closed his eyes and remembered 1963. He remembered the rush of joy when the team and fans emptied the dugout and the stands to celebrate the final out in the game that had given them the championship.

He opened his eyes. John True was still across

from him, smiling now. Dominic noted that the teeth on one side of his mouth were missing.

Then John True reached into his pocket and dropped a small shell necklace between them.

Dominic stared at the shells and then whispered, "It is September fourth. We are sixteen and a half games out of first place with only thirty-one games left to play."

John True reached across and took what was left of Dominic's beer.

He drank the beer down and said: "It can be done."

"What are your terms?" Dominic asked, without hesitation.

FRANK KING lives and works in Manhattan. He is the author of RAYA, NIGHT VISION, and the acclaimed DOWN AND DIRTY. As a youth he had major league baseball aspirations until he learned that the game's antagonism toward left-handed catchers was too deep-rooted.